D-H.
Bmc

WESTERN

TANNER

TANNER

by Lauran Paine

Walker and Company
New York

First published in the United States of America
in 1984 by the Walker Publishing Company, Inc.

Published simultaneously in Canada by John Wiley & Sons
Canada, Limited, Rexdale, Ontario.

Library of Congress Cataloging in Publication Data

Paine, Lauran.
    Tanner.

    I. Title.
PS3566.A34T3   1984   813'.54   83-40413
ISBN 0-8027-4034-0

Printed in the United States of America

10 9 8 7 6 5 4 3 2 1

Contents

I	A Woman and a Boy	1
II	An Old Phantom	9
III	Fear	18
IV	The Cave	27
V	After Nightfall	35
VI	Horses and Men	43
VII	The Ambush	55
VIII	Pursuit	65
IX	Skunked!	75
X	Someone's Error	85
XI	Thirty Feet of Freedom	96
XII	The Townsmen	107
XIII	One Day Later	118
XIV	Before Daylight	131
XV	A Hot Afternoon	138
XVI	Thunderhead Sky	145
XVII	The Agency	154

CHAPTER 1

A Woman and a Boy

The end of summer had its requiem in an explosion of color; it spread from tree to tree, from leaf to leaf, from hilltop to valley, from the towns out across the endless open range to the foothills, and higher to the vast backdrop of rough-textured mountains.

It changed the goldenrod, the blue sage, and dusty chaparral. It brought yellow shades to the birch; scarlet brilliance to the softwood trees: russet, burgundy, speckled crimson, and leathery brown to the oaks.

It provided perfect camouflage all along the lower foothills, and if, as was common during autumn, there was a little wind to create motion among the undergrowth and trees, it also provided something to conceal the movement of stealthy horsemen. All animals, including two-legged ones, watched for movement. It was the only thing that attracted attention in a world which was otherwise still.

The sky was moving, gray and troubled, pushed onward from north to south by a high, unheard strong wind that whittled and shaped the soiled clouds.

Smoke rising from chimneys barely cleared the tops before

it was whipped away and shredded. At ground level the wind was gusty and seemed to change direction, sometimes arriving from several ways at once, which made the gaunt woman and the gangling youth, who were pouring lye soap from iron kettles into molds, suspect that there actually would be no storm at all, just a lot of wind and a menacing sky on this gray, raw day.

They had been at the kettles since an hour after dawn. Making soap required time plus labor, and was only attempted when the signs were right. The gaunt woman, her thick graying hair held close by a blue bandana, worked with a powerful motion. She had been doing this for twenty years—longer if the times counted when, as a child, she had helped her mother.

Wind whipped wood-fire ash from beneath the cauldron. The woman paused to warm her chapped hands in an ankle-length apron, squinted at the sky, then gazed at the lanky boy who looked just like her, though she did not think so.

"Not till late tonight," she called against the wind. "But it's early, John. At least a month early."

The boy was using a threadbare cuff to wipe his face, watery from an ash that had hit his eyes. He did not respond, but poured the last of the hot soap, then put down the iron kettle and used both hands to wipe his face again. When he finished, he blinked and looked around in the direction of the sturdy log-walled house and beyond, to where the free flow of grassland ran. He showed the same strong features as the woman, although his black hair and dark eyes contrasted with her lighter hair and gray eyes. He was tall but still quite young, and when particularly strong gusts hit, he would brace against them, neither broad nor sturdy enough to stand unaffected.

They covered the molds on their sawhorse table with flat boards weighted down by rocks, then killed the fire with ash mixed into spring water and went into the log house.

Inside, except for a scraped rawhide windowpane, it was easier to ignore the wind. Heat from the mud-wattle fireplace made the house almost too warm, at least to people who had been out of doors. It was burning down to coals, so the woman said, "Fetch wood, John," and turned to the basin to scrub before starting their meal.

The gangling youth went to the roofed-over, three-sided big woodshed a few yards north of the house and briefly leaned to look out and around. He studied the sky and the eastern foothills, the farther-back tangle of crooked mountains, and listened to the wind whistle through knotholes at his back. Instinctively he felt kinship with the free wildness of the approaching storm.

He had been born back in Missouri but never knew any country other than this one, nor any other existence. He had arrived out here as a bundled baby. There had been no time for childhood. He had no regrets, because he did not know he was supposed to have them.

There were no children nearby, and he had learned to amuse himself without companionship. His father had left the high country to seek employment down around Denver —or any place he could find it.

On rare occasions, he and his mother hitched up and drove to Tomkinsville to get letters from his father, sometimes with money enclosed, and on those days they bought flour, baking soda, sugar, coffee, the barest staples, then drove back. John would see boys his own age, but he was never able to go talk with them.

The clouds were torn and tattered. They were a dirty shade of white with black edges. The clearings above them showed gun-metal gray, and if the sun was up there, it was completely obscured.

He watched the trees sway and twist, saw leaves falling, and when one of those abrupt silences arrived as the wind pulled back to leave everything still and motionless, he also

saw three riders moving in single file along the farthest foot-
hill ridge, passing in and out among flame-red sumac and
the patriarch black oaks, whose colors and motions had hidden the shapes and the movement of horsemen.

He watched, fading back a little into the shadows of the
woodshed. As a child he had learned to watch his parents;
when they had stood still, listening and looking, he'd also become still. He had grown to half manhood with a strong
streak of inherent wariness, for the homestead was isolated.
The nearest town, Tomkinsville, was eleven miles distant;
the nearest residence was the main house at Anchor Ranch,
six miles north and west. It might as well have been on the
moon. Anchor range men never came up the broad tongue
of land John's father had homesteaded. He had waved at
Anchor riders and they had never waved back. His father
had tried to explain. The Bancroft homestead was on land
that Anchor had used for many years, but even if it hadn't
been, if it had been some other place, the Bancrofts would
still be homesteaders—and range cattlemen had no use for
homesteaders.

But there had been no trouble. His father had said there
probably would not be—as long as the Bancrofts minded
their own business.

The wind returned, whipping around a corner of the shed
making the lodgepole rafters groan with its force. John
waited for the three riders to reappear through a grove of
wild maples whose golden shades were tinged with faint
pink.

It was a long wait; the horsemen did not reappear. John
guessed they had ridden down the far side of the slope, probably to escape the wind. He waited until his mother came to
the porch looking for him, then quickly made up an armload
of dry fir and headed for the house.

She held the door for him, then closed it, and as he placed

the chunks in the box beside the heath, she said, "Barley soup and loaf."

John smiled as he turned around. His mother could make food taste special out of just about anything she put her hands to. He had heard his father say that, and it was a fact.

"There were three riders on the ridge by those wild maples."

He watched for her reaction. She continued to slice the meat, so he relaxed a little, and when she offhandedly said, "Anchor, most likely—range men do a lot of saddlebacking in the autumn," he shed his coat and the old hat with a hole in the crown, and went to the basin to wash.

The only light came from a coal-oil lamp on the table. If the sun shone, then there was also a glow from the rawhide windowpane. He had watched his father stretch that piece of hide on a board and scrape it very carefully until it was paper-thin. In Tomkinsville there were glass windows, which permitted a view from inside or out. Rawhide panes admitted light but could not be seen through.

The wind died. John's mother instinctively waited for it to return. She carried two plates to the table and sat opposite her son. She raised a spoon, but stopped to watch her son.

The boy ate ravenously. He could eat like that at any time of day. Occasionally, his mother teased him about his appetite. She knew why he ate like that; his father was a tall, spare, hard-muscled man, who ate the same way. To the woman, the boy was very much like his father, including the dark hair and eyes. She saw none of herself in the lad.

The wind returned, slowly at first, then with increasing strength and malice. It shook the rawhide pane and scrabbled under the lodgepole eaves, making the kind of noise that set folks' nerves on edge.

When thick snow lay on the ground, people remained close by the hearth. When late-summer sun burned straight down, baking the earth to iron and sending cattle belly-deep into sump-spring mud, people went to the waterholes, too, and soaked in the tepid water. But wind was an enemy against which there was no defense for those who had to spend much of their time out in it.

His mother ate barley soup, watched her dark-eyed son, and eventually said, "There are no cattle in the hills east of here. If they would ride down here, I could tell them that."

John, who always ate meat first, pushed away the empty plate and pulled in his bowl of soup. As his father had once said with a twinkle in his eye, his mother's barley soup was too thin to plow and too thick to drink.

She ate a moment, then glanced at her son again. Loneliness was something she knew about. Its antidote was to keep busy. She kept busy and tried to keep her son busy. Someday, her husband would return. He had been gone almost a full year now; occasionally, at night, she would lie on her back in the big double bed he had made, with unshed tears in her eyes.

She had grown up with hardship, knew no other way of life, but there were times when her spirit longed terribly hard for a measure of softness. In Missouri, when her parents had been alive, there had been times—rare and therefore well remembered—when her father had driven back from town with a ribbon in his pocket, or when her mother had made her a calico dress.

John's head came up slowly, the spoon halfway to his mouth. He looked steadily at her. "That wasn't the wind."

She straightened up to listen but heard nothing. Still, danger was also something she knew about, so she rose and went to the rear door, leaned there briefly, listening, then reached with a roughened hand to lift the bar and ease the door back a trifle.

John stepped to the place where fireplace and log wall met, picked up the Springfield carbine leaning there, and soundlessly crossed toward the door. He was not quite seventeen, and he was frightened, but fear was not a new experience; he knew what people did under these circumstances. He obeyed instinct by easing back the heavy hammer, then watched as his mother leaned to peek outside. He held the gun barrel slanting floorward while he waited.

His mother stiffened, motionless for a long time over whatever she saw, and the cold coming through the cracked-open door made the fireplace flames gutter around their oak coals.

She opened the door halfway.

John saw the bent old man stumble past her, wrapped in a blanket with a shawl over the top of a ragged hat lashed beneath a brown, leathery chin. John raised the barrel slightly. Black eyes with muddy whites lifted from the gun to the boy's face and lingered as John's mother moved around the old man and said, ''Go by the fire,'' briskly gesturing in case he had not understood.

He was an Indian. Maybe not a full blood, but close to it. He obeyed, and John turned slowly in order to continually face the old man while holding the Springfield carbine in both hands.

She took him a bowl of hot barley soup. He was wearing gloves with all ten fingers sticking through. He was ragged and old, and when he sat down on the mud-wattle hearth and the dirty old threadbare blanket fell away, it was obvious he was unarmed.

His hair was a tangled gray with streaks of dark all through it. He had once been fairly tall but now was shorter, and his face was a patchwork of lines. John eased down the dog of the carbine and allowed it to sag in his hands, watching the old man spoon food into a nearly toothless mouth. He knew a little about Indians—no more than most youths his age knew. He had heard his share of stories about them.

And he had seen Indians, too, but never up close. A couple of months before his father had left, he had stood with his parents watching a straggling, noisy, disorganized band of them go streaming northward, a mile or so out across the Anchor range. His father had said they were probably heading for the mountains to make meat. It had been that time of year.

The old Indian finished the soup and handed John's mother the bowl. He said something indistinguishable. John was engrossed. He was also uneasy, and did not see his mother turn with the bowl in her hand and very slowly straighten up to her full height, as motionless as stone.

There were a pair of tall, durably raw-boned younger Indians standing silently in the doorway behind her son, and these Indians had guns in their fists.

CHAPTER 2

An Old Phantom

The same selfless instinct that motivates a sow bear or a bitch wolf motivates a woman. Whatever might happen to John Bancroft's mother was not going to happen to her son if she could protect him.

"Son," she said, "put the gun down."

He turned in surprise to look at her, and saw the two stalwart broncos in the doorway with guns in their fists. They were watching him from unblinking black eyes, their faces expressionless. Both were lighter in color than the old man at the hearth. They were as tall as John, but thicker, older, and more mature. They were bundled inside old blanket coats, and their shoulder-length hair was black and coarse. Their faces were windburned to a mahogany red, and their boots were cracked and muddy.

"John, *put the gun down!*"

Awkwardly, he moved to obey, then straightened around to face the pair. He could feel his heart beating fast.

Ten feet away, hands clenched in her apron and looking steadily at the Indians, his mother said, "What do you want?"

9

They stepped inside, and the last one closed the door and dropped the *tranca* into place. He then stepped around his companion and went to the old man at the fireplace. He swept back his old coat to holster the pistol, then picked up the threadbare blanket to rearrange it around the old man's shoulders.

The other buck loosened his coat, put up his weapon, then reached over to lift John's carbine, raise the trapdoor, and extract the big bullet. He leaned the weapon against the wall and dropped the bullet into his pocket.

He faced Rachel Bancroft and said, "The old man is sick. We've come a long way. He can't go no farther."

She had already made her assessment of the old bronco. "All right," she said. "Leave him here. It's not fit out for anyone, let alone a sick person." With the shock past, she was quite willing to believe this was why the Indians had stopped: out of concern for the welfare of the old man.

The Indian still over by the door showed nothing in his face when he said, "What will you do when they come for him?"

Unconsciously, Rachel relaxed her hands enough to wipe them on her apron. "Who? Who is coming for him?"

"They want us for driving some cattle," the bronco told her.

Rachel's brow clouded. "Are you talking about cattlemen?"

"Yes."

She went to the stove and stood with her back to its dwindling warmth. She looked at her son, who was pale and watchful. Finally, she said, "What will they do?"

The stalwart Indian did not hesitate. "Hang him."

She glanced at the old man, who was ill and wizened and threadbare. "How much time before they get here—those cattlemen?"

The Indian did not know. "Maybe today. Maybe tomorrow. . . . What will you do when they ride in?"

She brushed back a thick coil of hair before replying. "I . . . don't know. I don't know what I can do."

"Hide him."

She gave the bronco an impatient scowl. "Where? Do you see a loft? We have no cellar. If they're like the cattlemen we've seen out here and they're after you hard, they'll search under every board."

"They will kill him. He is old and sick."

She said dryly, "And he stole cattle."

"No! *We* stole the cattle. Some In'ians saw them comin' and told us. We got ready to run, and he came along."

"Why . . . is he your father?"

"Yes. If we left him, he would be alone. We tried to make him go back. . . . He didn't steal no cattle, but if they find him, they'll hang him from a tree."

Rachel looked helplessly at her son. Until then he had kept silent and listened. Now, interpreting her worried look as a plea, he said, "I can hide him, Ma."

She became irritable. "Where? Cattlemen don't set out after cattle thieves, Son, unless they mean to find them. If we're hiding him and they find it out—"

"They won't find him, Ma. I know a place they'll never find him."

The Indian standing at the fireplace with the old man had so far been silent. Now he turned and slowly considered the youth. He moved soundlessly toward John, dug in a pocket, lifted the boy's hand, and placed a small, heavy doeskin pouch on it. The drawstring of the pouch had been knotted and reknotted as though whoever had tied it had no intention of ever opening the pouch.

This Indian was leaner than his companion. His features were not as bitterly cast nor as hard. "Hide him," he told

John. "Maybe you have a good blanket to wrap him in. Give him something to eat."

Then they left.

Rachel stood looking at her son. He handed her the little pouch, which she turned and indifferently placed upon a shelf at her back next to the tins of flour, sugar, and coffee. She placed it in front of them, then turned and said crossly, "Why didn't you keep quiet? If range cattlemen find this old In'ian on our place . . . John, we only have the horse shed and the woodshed. Have you any idea what stockmen do to homesteaders who get mixed up in something like this?"

"Ma, we got all day today and maybe all tomorrow." He turned aside from her. The old Indian was holding his blanket close, black eyes watching them with almost animal intensity. John said, "Mister, can you walk a little?"

Rachel made that unconscious motion of drying her hands again. "He don't speak English, John. Those old ones hardly ever do." She clutched the apron. "Oh lord!"

"Ma, put the rest of the meat in a cloth. I'll fill one of the water bottles. Then I'll hide him." John went to the door. "It's gettin' dark out."

It was not quite four o'clock, but the storm had brought all its scattered dark clouds together into one lowering mass. It was as dark outside as it would have been at ten o'clock.

"Ma, put the meat in a cloth."

She roused herself and, with slumped shoulders, turned to obey. There was nothing left to say or do. The old bronco was there, his sons had departed, and whether she wanted to do it or not, her only recourse—unless she wanted man-hunting rangemen to find her with that old Indian in her house—was to help her son get him into hiding.

This was one of those times when she desperately needed her son's father at her side, but she knew he was not going to just show up.

She bundled the loaf, filled a bottle with hot barley soup,

and turned to watch her son strip a brown blanket from his bed and, after getting the old man on his feet, wrap it around him.

The old man's intense black stare was now aimed at her son. He made a toothless grin and uttered some guttural sounds. Rachel went over to hand them the bottle and bundle, then stepped to the door to peer outside. It was dark; a brawling wind and the metallic scent of brimstone added menace to the wild gloom.

She went to her bedroom, off the main room, dug out her husband's dragoon revolver with the long barrel, went over to where her son was steering the old man toward the door, and pressed the weapon into John's hand. Then she said, "Wait. I'll get my shawl."

He stopped her. "No. You stay inside. Stoke up the fire, Ma. It'll take me maybe an hour. Stoke up the fire and keep the door barred."

She lost sight of them by the log-walled horse shed. Inside, with the door closed and barred, she sank down at the table, put her head in her hands, and struggled unsuccessfully against the desolate feeling and the tears.

She had always been a praying woman. She had been raised that way, but over the last few years, with fewer and fewer clear answers, she had been praying less and working harder.

But she prayed now—though not with very much hope. When she had finished, there was no sensation of having been heard. When she had been a child, Jesus had been a friend. She and her ragdoll and Jesus had played, picked wildflowers and made mud pies together. That was so long ago. . . .

This morning she and her son had made soap under frustrating circumstances, battered by the elements, and her thoughts had been bitter.

Tonight she wished that come tomorrow, the usual miseries would be all they had to worry about.

Her son returned as the first large raindrops fell. He was slightly breathless, as though he had been running. She barred the door after him and turned up the lamp to see him better. He smiled broadly at her.

"Nobody'll find him, not unless I show 'em."

She stoked up the firebox of the stove and put soup on to heat. "Where did you leave him?"

"Remember I told you about a place I found in the foothills last spring when I was hunting sage hens?"

She did not remember but nodded her head.

"That's where I put him. He'll be dry and warm. It can rain a week and he won't get a drop on him. The roof of that old cave is solid stone. Two of the sides are, too." He went to the table, leaving his old hat and coat on the floor by the unloaded Springfield carbine, which had once been a military rifle but now had the barrel sawed off probably because that made it easier to carry the thing on horseback.

He smiled in triumph at her. "It's goin' to rain tonight, Ma. By tomorrow no one'll be able to find any tracks."

It did better than that. It not only rained most of the night, but it was still doing so long after a soggy, gray, and demoralizing dawn arrived.

Rachel was kneading up a fresh loaf while her son was having breakfast when she said, "How sick was he, Son?"

"I guess he's mostly just old, Ma. He's got a sort of stiff leg and can't walk real good . . . He was tellin' me something when I got him inside the cave. He didn't act real sick. He kept wanting to go look outside, and I had to keep shovin' him back and make him sit down. Then I wrapped him up and came on back. If no one rides in today, I'll go back up there tonight."

Rachel squeezed the loaf into its odd-shaped pan and

pushed it into the oven as she said, "This time I'll go with you."

Then she straightened around to gaze at her son. His eyes were bright—brighter than they had been in weeks. She wagged her head. What was it in men, even only half-grown ones, that seemed to make them happiest when they were doing something foolish?

He rose to take his empty bowl to her, smiling directly into her eyes. Just for a moment she was resigned, and then a startling thought occurred to her. Jesus *had* answered her prayers. He had answered them that dawn Rachel had been bedded to birth her child, and He had been answering them ever since, and she had been too preoccupied to realize it. He had let her watch her child grow, learn to laugh and work and face disappointment. He had given her something of which she would never tire.

She turned her back to John and bent as if to look at the meat in the oven, her eyes misted over.

John went to the shed to split rounds into stove wood, and Rachel put a fir knot in the fireplace. Listening to the eaves dripping, she began to bake; on this kind of a day there was little else to be done.

As for the Indian—her feelings toward Indians were not charitable. Her mother's brother had been killed by marauders in a plowed field in broad daylight, and she had seen the smouldering ruins of a wagon train of emigrants on her way west a few years back. Now, years later, she still remembered details of the slain people and animals with particular vividness. . . .

That the Indian was old and ailing meant nothing at all to her. She worked, filling the house with wonderfully tantalizing aromas, but she couldn't help thinking of the old man clutching blankets to his shriveled frame in a damp cave. She also recalled how the younger men had looked back at him before departing.

John returned, flushed from hard labor and smiling. He filled the woodbox, and when she gestured for him to be seated so she could feed him, she said, "We'll take something hot with us tonight. He's old, and its bound to be clammy in your cave. I'd take some of your father's whiskey, but. . . . Sit down, Son.

An hour after they had eaten, her spirits brightened. "No one with a lick of sense would be riding in this kind of weather."

John glanced up, smiling, not over what she had deduced but over something he had mentioned the day before and was still pleased about. "There's been enough rain to wash out elephant tracks."

But manhunters did not always go entirely by tracks.

John went down to the horse shed to fork timothy hay to their team animals, and, as he usually did when he was between chores, to stand in the doorway leaning on the fork handle, protected from the elements while he looked out and around at his isolated, lonely world.

Rain was still falling, but the drops were smaller and there was a lot less sound. It seemed to John as though they were now going to get one of those monotonous, steady downpours that sometimes lasted for days. He sniffed the air—and saw movement from the corner of his eye.

They were coming down out of the dripping trees and underbrush, one behind the other, shiny in saddle slickers, booted Winchesters slung forward from beneath *rosaderos,* hunched, their heads pulled low inside turned-up collars—six of them on horses that looked from a distance to be a uniform shade of wet black.

For a moment John had difficulty breathing, but then he flung aside the pitchfork and ran to the house, pushed his way inside, closed the door to lean upon it, and turned a white face toward his mother.

"They're comin' onto the meadow, Ma. Six riders, and they aren't from Anchor."

She plucked at her apron. "Six? For mercy sakes!"

"Yes'm. And they got Winchesters on their saddles."

She wiped, and rewiped, both hands on her apron. "Now you listen to me, Son. We don't have an In'ian here. They can look if they're a mind to. And they will. . . . John, unless you or I tell them, they aren't going to know, are they?"

He stared at her. "Tell them?"

"By the way we look an' act, Son, or by bein' careless in what we say, John, you remember this: It's not going to be just the old Indian, if they find we had him hid. Do you understand that?"

"Yes'm."

She impulsively crossed over and gathered him into her arms and held him tightly, then turned abruptly toward the stove as she said, "You have to make them believe you, Son. You got to show in your face that you don't know anything about any In'ians.

"It's play-actin', John. Don't overdo it. Just make it seem as natural as daylight. . . . Now look out there and see if they're still coming."

He cracked the door to peer out and, without drawing back, told her they were out of the trees now, heading straight across the clearing toward the house.

CHAPTER 3

Fear

The foremost rider was no more than average in height. He was thickly and powerfully put together and reminded John of the blacksmith over at Tomkinsville.

They sat their saddles with water dripping from hat brims, looking whisker-stubbled and uncomfortable. Several were older men. Two or three looked not much older than John, and none of them carried an extra ounce of meat.

The man with the blacksmith build said his name was Tanner. Then he smiled at Rachel and said he would be pleased to pay her for breakfast and a bait of hay for the horses.

She had both hands clasped inside her apron when she curtly nodded at Tanner. "John here will show you where to tether the animals out of the rain at the horse shed. . . . I'll make up a meal, Mr. Tanner . . . I'm interested in where you're from. You're not Anchor riders."

Tanner's reply was brief. "We come a considerable distance. From up north. We been five days on the trail of some cattle-stealing In'ians."

18

Rachael's gaze did not waver. "And they came down this way?"

"Yes'm." Tanner shifted his gray gaze to young John. "Come along, boy." He reined around in the direction of the horse shed, leaving Rachel to watch as her son tagged after them on foot. She went inside to start work and hoped very hard that her child would be equal to the challenge of the questions she was sure the strangers would ask.

Tanner dismounted under the shed's overhang and waited until his men were also on the ground. John showed them where they could tie their horses, then went inside and returned within moments with a fork full of fragrant timothy hay. He parceled it out to where the horses were tossing their heads impatiently, and he laughed at their motions.

Three of the riders took their saddles inside the shed to leave them upended, with blankets left sweat-side up to dry. They were sure-handed men, quiet, and obviously knowledgeable. When the other riders entered the shed, Tanner removed his gloves and watched John feed the horses. He said, "Where's your pa, son?"

"Working out. Down around Denver somewhere. Been gone about a year now."

Tanner accepted that. There was nothing unusual about homesteaders existing this way. First, the country broke their spirits when they attempted to farm it. Then, to avoid starvation, the man of the family desperately went in search of outside work, and finally, they heaved everything into a wagon, hitched up, and never looked back. The range country had scores of forlorn, dilapidated homesteader shacks, abandoned by people who had come west with great hope.

"Just you and your ma, boy?"

"Yes, sir."

"Hard hoeing, isn't it?"

"Yes, sir," answered John, "but we dug potatoes and got

turnips in the woodshed, and I hunt so's ma can put up meat.''

Tanner waited until John had finished with the feeding and was looking around to be certain each horse had enough, then said, "Any riders come through lately?"

John continued to look at the feeding horses. "No, sir. We're out of the way."

"What about that Anchor outfit your ma mentioned. Where is it?"

John pointed through the drizzling gray mist. "Northwest, about six miles."

"Cattle?"

"Yes, sir. It's owned by a man named Mr. Bent. He owns all the land you can see westerly from here. My pa says he's got thousands of acres—more than he can count. He's got lots of cattle and some herds of horses, too."

"Is he friendly to you folks, boy?"

John's arm dropped. "My pa says if we mind our own business, Anchor will get along with us. . . . Sometimes Anchor riders go past. Sometimes I wave, but they don't wave back. We mind our own business."

Tanner looked away as he said quietly, "I'm sure you do, boy. How long has your pa been gone?" His voice was sympathetic.

John made marks in the earth with the pitchfork tines. "Seems a lot longer'n a year, sometimes."

The other riders came out of the shed. From the direction of the house, they could pick up the aroma of cooking food, and one of them, about Tanner's size, but not as burly, turned a bronzed, weathered face and said. "Even if it's bear meat, I'll eat it."

John put aside the fork. "It's buck meat, and my ma's the best cook alive."

The older man ran a slow, rough glance up and down the boy. "I'll bet she is. What's your name, boy?"

"John. John Bancroft."

"Lead the way, John."

They trooped to the porch, shed their slickers, beat water out of their hats, shoved gloves under gun belts, and followed John inside.

The room had always seemed suitable when John and his mother shared it, but with six more people, it was barely large enough.

Rachel had set plates and cups around the old table. She glanced up once, then, with her lips compressed, motioned for the men to be seated. She brought them hot coffee—the last she had. Then she brought the big bowl of barley soup, and while they were eating that, she sliced the loaf and put the platter in the center of the table. She exchanged a searching look with her son, and he went over to stand beside her.

Tanner glanced up, smiling at Rachel. "The boy said you were the best cook around, ma'm, and he didn't stretch it at all."

She accepted the compliment without comment and turned to nudge her child. "More wood, John."

He left the room, and Rachel turned back to bank the stove fire. That older rangeman with the dark eyes and coppery, lined face turned to watch her for a moment before continuing with his meal. When he had finished, and when John was back tending the fire, the older man said, "Lady, my ma used to make barley soup like that. She'd send me'n my sister out to gather wild onions and sage and whatnot. She made the finest soup I ever ate. Yours ranks right up there with hers."

The other men were still eating when the older man rose, picked up his hat, and went outside onto the porch to roll a smoke. Later, all but the youngest rider and Tanner went out there. Those two did not smoke. The young man picked up the unloaded Springfield and casually examined it, then raised a quizzical gaze to John. "They ain't much use without a bullet in 'em."

John floundered, but his mother spoke sharply. "You can have accidents when they're loaded, mister."

The cowboy leaned the gun aside and went to stand wide-legged with his back to the hearth.

Tanner had a final cup of coffee, then stood up, too. "The lad didn't see any riders," he told Rachel. "I was wondering if maybe you saw any. It would have been maybe yesterday or the day before. Three In'ians; two young bucks and one old one."

She answered from over by the stove with her back to him. "No sir. Mr. Tanner, I haven't seen an Indian in more than a year. Maybe they didn't come down this far, or maybe they turned off. Did they know you was after them?"

"Yes'm, they knew. When you're trailin' In'ians, you can't keep it from them." Tanner turned, eyed the empty carbine briefly, then walked out to join the smokers on the porch.

John helped his mother clean up after the meal, and when the tall young man by the fireplace had also gone outside, John and his mother exchanged a glance. She forced a smile. "Were you all right at the shed, John?"

"Yes. Mister Tanner asked about Pa, how long he'd been gone and all."

"Did he talk about Indians?"

"No. Just about Pa and Anchor, and whatnot. I fed their horses. If they stay long . . . well, we only put up about as much hay as we figured the team would need through the winter."

She nodded absently; at this moment, hay was the least of the things on her mind.

The rain petered out, and a chilly, dank fog took its place, rolling up into the neck of land where the homestead was located.

The strangers were considerate, which was the custom. When she sent John for firewood later in the day, that older man with the weathered face cheerfully helped haul in a couple of armloads. He told Rachel his name was Frank Morrison. He was Tanner's top hand up north. Tanner, he said, ran a lot of cows and owned thousands of acres in the foothills sixty or seventy miles to the northeast—close to the reservation where those cattle-stealing Indians had been seen making their raid.

Rachel said, "How many cattle did they take, Mister Morrison?"

"Well, we found forty and drove 'em back, but we figure they'd maybe already salted down about another ten or so and burnt the hides."

"I thought Indians kept hides. Mr. Morrison, to make their clothing and moccasins from."

Morrison smiled. "Yes ma'am, they do. But not when the hides got brand scars on 'em."

Rachel accepted that and would have turned aside, but Frank Morrison was comfortable and willing to be neighborly. "We lose a few head every year. Will Tanner figures it's cheaper to let 'em get away with a few head than it would be go up there and raise hob. Then they'd maybe commence firing the buildings at night and running off horses. . . . But sixty head. . . ." Frank Morrison shook his head. "Will's a tolerant man. He'd have to be to run cattle up alongside an In'ian reservation, but this time they was off the reservation. The army wasn't interested, so it's up to us to teach 'em a lesson."

Rachel said, "Mr. Tanner's name is Will?"

"Yes'm. Mind telling me your name?"

Rachel looked steadily at the bronzed, loose-standing range rider. "It is Mrs. Bancroft, Mr. Morrison."

"That's a good boy you have, Mrs. Bancroft. . . . I was married once. We had a daughter." Morrison's expression changed slightly as he headed for the door. Rachel watched him, expecting more, but he went outside without another word.

Tanner was waiting with Sal, the tall, younger man who had warmed his backside at the hearth a little earlier. "Maybe the woman's right," he said to Morrison. "Maybe they turned off somewhere. Sure as hell their horses are rode down and they've got to find ways of favoring them."

Morrison stood waiting.

"You and Carl could get onto that ridge yonder and make a sweep southward. If they were still going in that direction, Frank, they left some sign after the rain. I'll ride over and talk to the feller at that neighboring cow outfit, in case they turned off and left cover to maybe steal fresh animals, or just to cross open country in a storm so's we couldn't see them or pick up their tracks."

Frank Morrison fished for his makings and systematically rolled a cigarette. He had worked for Will Tanner eleven years. He was top hand and probably would have been range boss if Tanner did not do that job himself. They were long-time associates and friends. Frank had been speaking his mind for eleven years, and he spoke it now. "You might leave someone here, Will."

Tanner's eyes narrowed. "What for?"

Morrison exhaled blue smoke. "Well, maybe put some-one over yonder up through the trees out of sight of the house. . . . It's nothing, just a feeling I got. . . . Come along, Carl, let's get rigged out and up atop that ridge."

Tanner lingered on the porch watching Morrison and the younger man cross to the horse shed. He blew out a big breath and went over by the woodshed, where his riders were sitting on fir rounds feeling replete and comfortable.

He told them they would ride over and hunt up that An-chor cow outfit and ask some questions. Then he pointed to a man named Dutch Meier and said, "You ride out with us, then cut off when we get the trees between us and the cabin. Keep out of sight, but ride back up near that ridge we came off of, and keep watch on the house."

Dutch chewed tobacco. He sprayed amber then eyed his employer behind the half droop of his lids. "Somethin' goin' on, Will?"

Turner turned his head in the direction of the horses as he grumpily replied, "Some damned notion of Frank's."

"He seen something, or what?"

Tanner's annoyance made him give a short answer. "You know Frank as well as I do. He gets some damned idea and gives out little pieces of it. Anyway, we don't need for all of us to hunt up this cowman. The lad offered a fair idea of where the home ranch is."

One of the others raised his head. "Where are Frank and Carl going?"

They all turned now to watch the pair ride out from the vicinity of the horse shed, which was a little distance southwest of the log house and the woodshed.

"To look southward for sign," replied Tanner, and headed for his outfit so he could saddle up. The others rose and trooped along in his wake, and Rachel, who had been watching from the doorway, eased the panel closed when the men disappeared inside the shed, turned toward her son, and said, "I think they're leaving, Son."

John's brows dropped. "Mr. Tanner said he'd pay us, Ma."

Her answer was cynical. "They always tell you that—I'll gladly let that go just to see them leave John, in a couple of hours they'll be far enough off so's we can go up to your cave."

She sighed and went to the hearth to sit with her back to the firelight. Her son cracked the door a few inches and peered out. He watched a long time, then very quietly closed the door and turned, looking puzzled. "They aren't goin'

southward, Ma; they're heading off in the direction of Anchor.''

She considered that for a moment and came up with a
good guess. "They'll go talk to Mr. Bent or his men about
three Indians passing across the open range yesterday.
That's a twelve-mile ride, Son. . . . I guess they aren't
leaving, which means they'll be back tonight, most likely,
Son, if we're going to look after that old Indian, we'd better
go right now.''

"It's still light out, Ma.''

"John, after they return, we won't be able to go. Right
now, and for the next few hours, we'll be safe with them up
at Anchor.'' She rose. "I'll get my shawl. There's some barley soup left. Put it in a bottle and we'll take it up there with
us.''

CHAPTER 4

The Cave

The fog was thin and wet—more nearly a mist, actually—and went right through their clothing, but neither John nor his mother noticed as they crossed the yard with long strides.

Somewhere above, the sun was trying hard to burn off the mist. It would succeed, but not for an hour or so, and then the land would steam.

John slackened his pace only when his mother fell slightly behind. Her long skirt hampered movement, otherwise she would have been able to easily keep abreast of him. She was a rawhide-and-sinew woman, worked down to bone and muscle, but above all, she had a particular hardihood of spirit; she had been born with some of it, and her life since marriage had instilled the rest.

John was also tough and durable, but he had youth in his favor. He never seemed to tire. He had been hunting in the foothills and farther mountains since he had been fourteen, could run up a steep hill, or split felled timber all day long with an even, powerful swing.

When they reached the first rise, with its wet, lustrous undergrowth and trees, John stopped to look back. His mother also turned. There was no movement. She gathered her wet skirt and looked around. "How much farther, Son?"

"Maybe a mile or less. You want to rest?"

"No. Don't worry about me. I was loping over hills bigger than these before you was born." She smiled, he smiled back, and they hastened ahead, zigzagging now because of the undergrowth and timber.

The cave was invisible from the front, where wild grapes grew and three bull-pines dripped water. He pointed into the gloomy shade. "Beyond the bushes. You see the opening?"

She had to edge around a big tree to make it out. "How did you find it, John?"

"Last winter I was tracking a raccoon that was dragging one of my traps. He went in there."

They had to step carefully to avoid getting wetter than they already were. The cave was not quite tall enough to permit them to stand erect, and it had a moldy scent, along with an even stronger, ranker smell. Rachel stopped in the entrance to peer through the gloom. She wrinkled her nose and said, "Bear cave."

Her son scoffed. "Naw; there wasn't anything in here."

"Maybe not now, Son, but there has been. I've been in bear caves before. I know the smell."

The old man was sitting wrapped in his blankets, watching them. They had soggy daylight behind them, but his eyes were accustomed to the shadows. He coughed and spoke gutturally. When they approached, he held up one finger and made a gesture around it with his other hand.

John did not understand, but his mother did. "Candle, Son. We should have brought some candles." She knelt and studied the old Indian. He did not seem any worse than when she had first seen him in the cabin. She handed him the bottle of warm barley soup. He tipped back his head and drank nearly all of it, then leaned the bottle against rough stone where the other two bottles, both empty, were also leaning.

Rachel said, "He's out of water."

John picked up the empty water bottle. "There's a spring north of here in a berry thicket. I'll fetch him some."

Rachel got into a more comfortable position facing the old Indian. He smiled, showing a few snags of teeth, and began telling her something of which she did not understnad a single word. He paused, evidently saw her blank expression, and raised his hands to repeat himself, using *wibluta*.

Because she could make no sense of sign language either, she shook her head.

The old man dropped both hands to his lap and simply sat there looking at her. Then he reached for one of her hands, turned it palm upward, placed his own rough hand palm downward over it, and smiled again.

She smiled back, believing she understood that this touching of palms meant friendship, which it did.

The sun finally burned away the mist, and a little later its heat burning against the ground made steam arise. It was possible, finally, to see a little better inside the cave, and when John brought back the refilled water bottle, the old Indian made a clear gesture for him to sit down beside his mother. Then he repeated the palm touching, which to Rachel and her son simply meant that the old bronco was grateful, but it meant more than that; it signified a promise of life-long remembrance for a good service rendered, and lasting friendship as well.

They departed when the old Indian looked tired. Outside, there was sticky heat all the way back to the cabin. It would last only until sundown, which was close by the time they got back. It might return the following day; autumn was the most unpredictable season of the year.

Rachel drank from the dipper and bucket, and mopped sweat from her forehead. She smiled at her son. For no fathomable reason, she felt much better than she had felt for the past few days.

"He looks fine," she told her son. "I didn't expect that; him cooped up in the damp old cave and it storming all the while—him being old an' all."

"That's how they live, Ma. I've seen pictures of 'em standing to their hocks in snow holding a blanket around 'em without a shirt or anything, naked from the middle up."

She said, "You better fork feed to the horses, Son, and I'll start a meal." She looked at him steadily, with deep and abiding affection in the depth of her eyes. "I'm proud you'd help an old Indian."

He went across the porch on his way to feed, and Rachel watched his supple stride and tall body. His father had been like that, too, once—a mite thicker through the shoulders and chest, but then, the boy was still shy of seventeen.

The sun dwindled. Long summer evenings had been gone awhile, and in their place a quick chill arrived now, within moments of the time the sun departed.

Horses sweated more in autumn because they were already getting winter hair. It was common among range men never to work a horse hard if he had to dry out after sundown. Distemper killed a lot of good horses.

Tanner would have preferred to cover the distance back from the Anchor outfit swiftly, but he did not do so. He told himself they would eat breakfast at the homesteader's place, and then, if Frank had found nothing, they would turn back. He did not want to give up the hunt, for it was against his nature to abandon any course, but he knew what his riders were thinking—that he had pushed this stubborn wish to hang some cattle thieves beyond the point of common sense. Frank, in particular, felt that way. Tanner knew his top hand as well as Frank knew his employer.

They had plenty of work to do back on their home range in

order to get ready for the approaching winter. And these damned Indians were giving them one hell of a run for their money.

Ranging a long glance toward the forested slope north of the wide spit of land where the Bancroft place was, he saw a solitary horseman picking his slow way among the multi-colored trees and bushes.

Briefly, he speculated that Frank and Carl had returned by now. Behind him a rider said, "Hey, there's Dutch."

But they did not rendezvous for another half hour, and by then the sun was gone and a dwindling long red streak across a cold-looking sky reflected what little light was left.

Dutch pulled up, sank both gloved hands to his sad-dlehorn, and gazed steadily at Tanner. "They got an In'ian hid in a cave about a mile or so from their log house."

Tanner reached to turn his collar up. "Did you see him?"

"Naw. I saw them go back up in there from the house about an hour or so after you left. I sidled down as close as I dared and heared the woman talkin' inside the cave. Then the boy went to a spring and filled a bottle with water and took it back into the cave."

"How do you know it was an In'ian?"

"I could smell the bastard. I wasn't goin' to poke my head in the openin' with the sun at my back for him to blow my brains out."

Tanner sat in thought for a moment before speaking again. "All right. Take us up there, Dutch. Go the way you came down here so's they can't see us from the house." He turned toward the hard, weathered faces behind and knew he didn't have to say anything about being careful or quiet.

Meier did even better. Rather than return along the for-ested ridge, he led them back down along the north slope of it, where they would be completely out of sight.

Not a word was spoken until they emerged around the

thick haunch of their hill and one of the men behind Tanner said, "Yonder's Frank and Carl."

They halted to watch as a pair or horsemen came angling up from the south, working their way through undergrowth into the open. It was really too shadowy to be certain that that was who the distant riders were, but the watching men all recognized the horses and the way the pair of men straddled them.

"Goin' to the house," Dutch Meier mused, and gazed at Tanner for instructions.

For a while Tanner watched the riders in silence, then gestured for Dutch to continue onward.

Where he felt it would be safe to dismount and leave the horses, Meier swung off and went to loop his reins over a low limb. He then lifted out his saddle gun and walked back to wait for the others. When they were together, he gestured with his carbine.

"Yonder in them red bushes in where the boy filled his bottle. I was holding my breath. He was behind me, an' if he'd been looking close, he'd have seen me sure as hell."

Tanner brushed this aside. "Where's the cave?"

Meier swung the carbine a little. "See them big pine trees? In behind them somewhere. I watched the lad walk past them, turn to his left, then he disappeared."

One of the men grounded his Winchester, staring toward the pines and looking doubtful. "Hell, Dutch, he could have turned off toward the house. There's so much underbrush down there."

"Naw, he didn't turn toward the damned house," exclaimed the indignant rider. "Him and his ma come out of there maybe ten, fifteen minutes later, an' I could see them all the way down to the open country. Afterward they went back to the house." Meier shifted his glare from the skeptical man back to Tanner. "Then I snuck in as close as I could—and I smelt an In'ian."

Tanner twisted to look toward the house and saw his other two men on the ground around their horses at the shed. He looked upward to where the last of the daylight was fading fast, and said, "Let's go."

They were more careful now. When they were still a half dozen yards from the cave, Tanner paused to glance up the eastward slope. There had been *three* Indians, not just one. He softly said, "Dutch, take someone with you and scale up that hill. I don't like the idea of us being down in this little draw if there's one in the cave and two more up yonder."

Meier and another man turned to start up through the brush and trees, halting frequently, not entirely because they were wary, but because as lifelong horsemen they did not have the kind of wind men needed to climb hills.

It was getting darker by the minute. Tanner's caution increased along with the diminishing visibility. He was certain of one thing; the Indians knew he was hunting them, and they also knew what he would do if he caught them. If they were run to ground, they could lose nothing Tanner did not intend to deprive them of anyway, so they would fight.

He hoisted the Winchester and held it across his body in both hands, and when he was less than three yards from the nearest bull-pine, he cocked it. Around him, the other men did the same.

They reached spongy layers of needles, where every footfall would be muffled, and finally saw the opening. It looked black. One man leaned, touched Tanner's arm and, when the cowman turned, pinched his nose with two fingers to indicate that he smelled an Indian.

There was one sure way to get that Indian. Step up to the opening and spray lead inside as fast as they could lever up and squeeze off bullets.

An older man tapped Tanner's shoulder and made a gesture to indicate speaking, and Tanner scowled. "You can't talk one out if he's forted up."

"A man can try," whispered the range rider. "If we start shooting, and the other two ain't also in there, they'll hear it and we'll be another week tryin' to catch up with them.

Tanner yielded with a curt nod, and the older cowboy eased up within a couple yards of the black hole, crouched slightly, and said something in a guttural, resonant rush of sound.

Moments passed. The old cowboy sank to one knee leaning on his Winchester. There was not a sound, then a quavery answer came from the depths of the cave, and the cowboy pushed upright and glanced over his shoulder.

The other men crept closer, a wary foot at a time. The older cowboy called into the cave again, then leaned to whisper to Tanner.

"It's the old one. He thinks I'm one of his sons."

Another quavery call came from within the cave, more insistent this time. The cowboy craned to peek inside but did not move any closer. Tanner nudged the man, and the cowboy spoke back to him. "He says for me to come inside. That he's got some soup to eat."

The range man handed Tanner his carbine, lifted out his Colt, and started ahead. He hung briefly just beyond the opening for a moment, raising his gun hand, then ducked down and entered the cave, unable to see clearly until he got close to the old man and could hear his breathing. The Indian did not move. The cowboy reached, caught a handful of blanket with one hand, and, with the other hand, pushed his six-gun straight at the old man as he cocked it.

CHAPTER 5

After Nightfall

Frank Morrison sat at the table watching Rachel Bancroft make herb tea. He had been wet and cold most of this day. Even the brief interlude of warm weather in late afternoon had not winnowed out all the chill in his bones. Frank had not been a young man for quite a few years. Outwardly, he was like rawhide, capable of doing anything younger range men could do. Inwardly, when he had sunk into slumber many a night at the Tanner bunkhouse or beneath a camp wagon, he'd been aching in every joint and muscle.

It was blessedly warm and peaceful in the cabin, and Frank drowsed until the woman said, "How do you know it was Indians, Mr. Morrison? South of here, the closer you get to Tomkinsville, there are lots of folks riding around on horseback."

Frank, with his back to the hearth, his old hat on the floor at his feet, his body loosening an inch at a time, answered slowly. "Well, there's ways of telling In'ians from whites, Miz Bancroft. But even if there wasn't, the way In'ians just naturally ride to keep out of sight. . . . And the place where they stopped to rest their animals, they left remnants of

35

In'ian grub. It was them all right. But somewhere along the way they lost one."

She turned to hand him a cup of herb tea without meeting his gaze. "It's hot. Let it set for a spell." She looked around as her child and the raw-boned, tall cowboy called Carl came in out of the settling dusk with armloads of firewood.

As the younger men noisily dumped wood into the woodbox, she dried both hands on her apron and said, "How far was it, Mr. Morrison?"

He was blowing on the tea. "Quite a distance. We saw rooftops on our left and southward. I guessed that'd be your town."

She nodded. "Tomkinsville; you covered a fair amount of distance goin' down there and coming back." She returned to the stove for two more cups of tea. "Round trip, you'd have covered about eighteen miles. That's a good day's ride, especially in this kind of weather."

He tasted the tea and privately wished she had put some whiskey in it. But it was hot, and the warmth was good all the way down, even without liquor. "We figured it was about that far, ma'am."

She put two more cups on the table for her son and the young cowboy. "You rode back eight or nine miles, Mr. Morrison, and if those were your Indians, they're still heading south."

Frank's steady, shrewd dark eyes went to her face. "So you figure they're beyond catching range."

She turned to meet his somber gaze. "Don't you, Mr. Morrison?"

"No ma'am. They've been a lot farther ahead of us than that and we've come up onto them. In something like this, Miz Bancroft, it's not a horse race; it is a wearing-down manhunt." Humor showed in his gaze. "I've done this before. It usually ain't the horses at all. It's who can go longest without sleep and something to eat."

"Indians are good at those things, Mr. Morrison."

His lined features reflected some tolerant inner thoughts. She was a woman; sometimes a man had to explain things to women the same way he did to little children. "All my life, folks have been telling me things like that, Miz Bancroft. I'll tell you somethin' to go along with it I learned when I wasn't much older'n your boy. There's never been an In'ian born who could outlast a range man. Maybe he can cover his sign and sneak around and cut back an' all, but I've yet to see one that can outride or outlast a range man. . . . And I've seen a few try it. . . . That tea was almighty good. My wife made 'arb tea like this. She'd put a little rosemary and blue sage in it. Just the littlest pinch." He paused, then added, "And a dram of whiskey."

For a moment Rachel held her clasped hands across her middle, then wordlessly went over to the high shelf, pushed aside the little doeskin pouch with its double-knotted drawstring, lifted down the jug, and returned to the table. She put it down in front of Morrison.

He looked from her to the jug, pulled the cob stopper, tipped whiskey into the bottom of his empty cup, shoved the jug toward Carl, and smiled. "Corn. I admire your husband for bein' a man who knows the difference between corn squeezings and rye whiskey, Miz Bancroft. There's rye and malt, but corn whiskey is best for a person." He watched Carl pour, and said, "You better go easy with that stuff. For awhile you'll be setting there in your chair, then you'll attempt to stand up and fall flat on your face."

She retrieved the jug away the moment Carl pushed it aside, placed it back up on the high shelf, and glanced over Carl's bent head at her son. His whiteness told her all she had to know; out in the woodshed Carl had told her son they'd found the trail of the two young Indians.

John had not touched his tea.

Carl drank deeply and blew out a big breath, rolled his

eyes around to Frank, and gave his head a wag. The older range man laughed and shoved both legs under the nearby table. It was mighty pleasant in the house with heat on his back from the hearth and whiskey in front of him. He sipped, and when Rachel offered to dilute the liquor with more tea, he shook his head. He could have told her that herb tea had always worked on him as a diuretic, except that he did not know the word, and the one he did know was never to be used in front of womenfolk.

John straightened and turned his head. A moment later they could all hear horses down by the shed, and Rachel crossed to the door to peer out. It was too dark to make much out, but the sounds were familiar ones as men cared for their horses and equipment.

She left the bar down but closed the door as she turned back. "Mister Tanner, most likely. I can't imagine it being anyone else. He's had a long day of it, up to Anchor and back. I don't know that he'll have got much help up there. They're not helpful people."

Frank sighed, drew in his legs, and rose. It required a moment for his joints to lock in and adjust, and in that length of time the door was thrust open as Will Tanner stamped in out of the cold, gloved and with his coat buttoned.

The remaining range men trooped in behind him, all of them glancing once at Rachel Bancroft, then avoiding another glance as they went across to the fire to stand stonily silent and waiting, while they shucked gloves and opened their coats to the blessed heat, seemingly oblivious to everyone and everything but the fire.

Tanner nodded at Frank and Carl, loosened his coat, and shoved his riding gloves into a coat pocket. He tipped back his hat and said, "Find anything, Frank?"

Morrison related all that he knew while Rachel, with a sudden knot in her stomach, went after more tin cups and more tea. She had a bad premonition. All she knew about

Tanner was that he was a direct individual, but not impolite. Just now he had entered her house, glanced at her once without offering any greeting—not even a perfunctory one—and was standing there now without removing his hat or shedding his coat. His men were acting the same way. They avoided looking at Rachel or her son.

She had never underestimated Tanner; she had feared the man from the moment he had appeared in the yard, sitting on his horse and looking at her.

Filling the cups provided her with something to do while Frank talked on. She took the cups to the expressionless, silent men at the hearth, met their wordless, grave nods of appreciation, then turned to ask Tanner if he'd care for some herb tea.

His reply was slow in coming. He was standing directly behind her son, giving her the same dispassionate gaze his men had showed. "No thank you, Miz Bancroft. If you'll step out to the porch with me, I'd like to show you something."

John could see the stain of spreading fear come into his mother's face and leaned to rise. Tanner put a strong hand on the boy's shoulder, forcing him to stay seated. "Set, boy," he said, then moved to hold the door for Rachel.

She was clutching her apron in both hands when she stepped out onto the porch.

It was dark out with a little skiff of a cold ground wind blowing. The old Indian was lying there in his two blankets. In the poor light, he resembled an untidy mound of soiled laundry. Her breathing stopped for a moment, then she went over and knelt to gently turn the old man face up. A pair of intent, unblinking black eyes stared up at her. The old man's nearly toothless mouth was pulled flat in a ragged, hard line. As they exchanged a long look, Tanner said, "That's one of them."

He had not raised his voice. She kept her back to him and

tried to make one of the old blankets into a pillow. The old man resisted her touch, and it dawned on her that he believed she had sent the range men to find him in the cave. She rocked back on her heels, let her hands lie quietly in her lap, and softly shook her head. It was the only thing she could think to do to convey to the old man that she had not betrayed him.

He stared steadily at her, then turned his head away so he would not have to look up at her, and Tanner spoke quietly again.

"He wouldn't believe you didn't help us find him even if he could understand English."

Rachel rose and straightened the apron before speaking to the range cattleman. "How did you find him; was he outside the cave?"

"No, he was inside. . . . I left a rider back on the hill to keep watch." Tanner looked steadily at her. "He's goin' to stay here while we go after the other two. I'll leave Dutch and Carl."

She could see his face passably well in the feeble starlight. There was no anger showing, or indignation, or even contempt for her clumsy attempt at hiding the old Indian, and that added to her fear.

On the eastward passage she had witnessed two camp trials both for killings. Both times, she had seen ash wagon tongues hoisted into the air and lashed back because they had been in treeless country, and she had seen the identical detached, expressionless looks on men's faces those times, too, when they had gagged, bound, and hanged both killers, leaving them suspended in the air while they convulsed at the height of the wagon tongues.

"Mr. Tanner . . . I didn't have any idea. . . . They said someone was hunting them, but I had no idea you'd be along during that storm. And this old man—"

His answer was in an expressionless tone. "You knew who

they were, ma'am. You know the penalty for stealing livestock. You been out here long enough to know that.'' He
stood poised to say more, but did not do so.

"Mr. Tanner, he is an old man, crippled in one leg, and
he's sick.''

Tanner gazed at her for a moment longer, then started to
turn toward the doorway.

She stopped him. "He didn't steal any cattle. He's the father of the two who did.''

"Is that what they told you?''

"Yes. They said they'd been warned you were coming
and saddled up to ride away, and the old man would not let
them go without him. They tried to make him go back. He
got a horse and followed them—they said they were all he
had, and if something happened to them he would be
alone—starve, most likely, Mr. Tanner. . . . Whatever
you got in mind, my child and I can't stop you, but how can
an old man like him be anyone's enemy? He can't ride, he
can hardly walk, he's sick and he's very old.''

Tanner looked down where the old Indian was lying. The
old man had not moved or turned his head. A true Indian,
regardless of the desperation in one of the voices behind him,
and the coldness in the other voice, he had detached himself.
Whatever pain and sorrow was in his heart, and regardless of
how his bent and scarred body hurt, he was already moving
away.

Tanner raised his eyes, considered Rachel Bancroft
briefly, then buttoned his coat and went to the open door to
poke his head in and say, "Frank—all of you but Dutch and
Carl—let's saddle up. Carl, you and Dutch stay here and be
damned sure you get every gun they got, and don't let either
of 'em go anywhere without one of you being along. *Anywhere!* And toss the old buck onto some blankets near the
fire. . . . When we come back I want him alive to see us
hang his sons.''

The men were pulling on gloves and buttoning coats as they trooped stonily down across the porch into the yard. Not one of them looked at Rachel as they stamped past.

Her son came to the door and waited until the men were halfway across the yard, then went to his mother's side. She put an arm across his shoulders.

Dutch and Carl came to the doorway, blocking the light from inside. One took the old man's ankles and the other one took his shoulders. He was light enough for either one of them to have lifted easily. As they straightened up, Dutch jerked his head. "Inside ma'am. You too, boy."

CHAPTER 6

Horses and Men

It was not as cold as it had been the previous night, but it still lacked a lot of being warm, and Frank Morrison rode resignedly; he would have preferred to have been one of the men left behind. An hour farther down the trail he turned drowsy. Maybe that was a result of the interlude of complete relaxation back at the cabin, and maybe it was the whiskey. He told himself it was some of each, but there was another, less welcome, thought in the back of his mind. He'd gotten drowsy other nights on the trail, too. It was age. Pure and simple, that's what it was.

Tanner roused Frank from his reverie with a question. "You thought they knew something, didn't you?"

"Sort of. Did you look at that shelf beside the cook-stove where those jugs and bottle were?"

"No."

"There was an In'ian medicine pouch up there. The drawstring was double-knotted the way they sometimes do with their medicine bundles."

Tanner regarded his top hand with mild skepticism. "You figured they'd been here from that?"

Frank shifted slightly in the saddle. "No, not exactly. But the lady said they hadn't seen an In'ian in a year, an' the pouch was settin' in front of the jugs and bottles. That soup she gave us . . . the barley was in a big bottle behind the pouch."

Tanner rode along for a while thinking about that, and eventually he shot a sidelong glance at Morrison. They had known each other a long while, and Frank had surprised him like this before. He fished for some jerky, which was covered lightly with lint from his coat pocket, and offered a stick, but Frank was comfortable and shook his head.

The moon arrived, along with a slight drift of long, narrow clouds from the east. It was a bright enough night. The other men talked a little, but only sporadically. They, too, had jerky, which was tough stuff to chew while carrying on a conversation.

The ridge began to peter out into a long decline about two miles south of the Bancroft place, but the undergrowth did not diminish, nor did the forested slopes around them. Even when they encountered flatter land, the mountains on their left held steady until Frank angled a little westerly and raised a gloved hand to point.

"If they camped, they'll be maybe five, six miles ahead, and, I'd guess from the tracks we found, a little to the west. To the east there's no trees nor decent cover; the farther along we ride in that direction, the less cover there is, but soon we'd ought to be able to see some town lights."

Tanner was not interested in town lights. "What I'd give a good horse to know," he said, "is whether or not they camped."

Frank thought they had. He had ridden over most of this ground earlier and had drawn some conclusions on that ride. "They're atop some pretty bad-off horses, Will. They know as well as anyone does that if a man has a horse drop under him he's on foot. Maybe they could afford to have that happen to them at other times, but they sure as hell can't let it happen this time."

The men continued along in silence for sometime. Once, a cougar screamed somewhere in the mountains, and for a while after all their mounts were a little high-headed and had a spring to their steps.

The cold gradually increased, and by the time they could make out the lights of a distant town to the south, Frank was bundled inside his coat, trying to imagine where the fugitive redskins could be.

Probably somewhere in the timber and brush to the west, while still heading southward. But where? There was something worse than having a horse drop under a man. It was stumbling onto a fugitive camp and having a horse shot out from under him.

He halted and sat awhile studying the country. No land forms looked the same in daytime as they did at night. He finally jutted his jaw in the direction of the timbered flatlands to their right. "They're either over there, or they're somewhere close to that town trying to steal fresh horses. We can sweep through the timber toward the town an' maybe kill two birds with one stone."

Tanner was a logical man. He looked from the timbered country toward the distant lights. "If they get fresh horses," he said, "we might just as well swap ends and go home . . . unless we get fresh horses too. . . . I think we'd ought to head for the town, Frank. I'll tell you why—because even if they aren't down there, we'll still be parallel with 'em, and on fresh mounts we can cut westerly and get below them before daylight. They can camp and rest for what's left of the night—we won't."

They turned toward Tomkinsville with Frank rubbing his stubbly jaw because he was not sure he agreed with all that Tanner had said.

The lights kept pulling away the closer they got to them;

the damned town was farther than it had looked. By the time they had the back lots and outskirts in sight, town dogs had detected a scent and were caterwauling.

Once they found the north stage road and got onto it riding southward, there were a lot fewer lights showing in Tomkinsville. It was not only late, but cold, too.

They rode at a slogging walk past tarpaper shacks, past half-log structures that had been part of the original Tomkinsville settlement, and saw a light here and there.

At the jailhouse a light burned, and over on the front wall of a log saloon, a pair of carriage lamps bolted on each side of the locked doorway seemed to be giving off about as much oily smoke as light. If people didn't keep the wicks trimmed, that was what happened. But the brightest glow came from down at the livery stable, which was also Tomkinsville's trading barn. There were two large lamps out front, and the doorless wide front opening revealed two more glowing from hanging wires above the wide earthen runway.

That was where they found four men in a cluttered room playing poker in a haze of smoke from the wood-stove and strong cigars.

Harnesses hung from wall pegs, saddles were piled atop cedar racks nailed to the walls, and old blankets, mostly stiff with dried horse sweat and matted hair, lay in a corner where an old brown dog was sleeping soundly.

When Tanner and Frank walked in with the other men behind them, those four poker players, who had heard nothing, looked up in surprise. Tanner nodded around as he squinted into the light while removing his gloves. "Evening, gents. Does one of you run this place?"

A paunchy older man chewing a dead cigar nodded his head, and cast his small eyes over the beard-stubbled, strangers. "Me," he said. "Jake Teale. This here is my night man. He'll take care of your horses. Arlo!"

A thin man with red splotches on his face and watery eyes stood up, nodding his head.

Tanner ignored the hostler. "Mr. Teale, we need four fresh horses, to buy."

The poker players stared. They'd had a little time to reach conclusions about these hard-looking men who had come in out of the late, cold night in need of fresh horses.

Jake Teale put down his cards and struggled up out of the chair. "Well now, gents," he said heartily, then cleared his throat before continuing, "It's a mite late. . . ." Teale breathed with some difficulty. He had dark shadows under his eyes, and there was a brown stain on his lips around the cigar. His look had the veiled, foxy brightness of a predator.

Tanner knew Teale's type. They all knew it. Teale was a horse trader all the way through. Every town in cow country had a Jake Teale.

He picked up a filthy old threadbare red and black coat and pulled it on as he said, "Trouble is, gents, I got mostly livery horses to rent out. We took most of the horses out to pasture yestiddy for a rest. All I got is a few sale horses, and most likely you boys wouldn't be able to. . . . Well, come along an' I'll show you what's here."

Teale had looked larger sitting at the poker table than he looked when he was standing up and moving. He stepped outside the harness room and coughed hard for a moment, then caught his breath in deep-down sweeps and started across to the far stalls, speaking as he went.

"I got a hell of a fine big sorrel horse in this stall. He's faster'n lightning and tougher'n a boiled owl. A man could ride him from Tomkinsville plumb to the Mex border and he'd only have to stop once in a while to catch a fresh breath. . . . You can't see in there."

Teale took a rope shank off a nail and entered the stall, talking quietly as he did so. The horse he led out was indeed powerfully put together, with a deep chest and thick forelegs. Teale turned him so they could see him better, then smiled at Tanner. "Mouth him, mister. The freighter I bought him off called him six. Go right ahead, mister, I ain't like some folks—I don't get indignant when fellers want to mouth them."

Tanner lifted the side of the sorrel's mouth, caught his tongue, pulled it out, and when the horse opened wide, Tanner and Frank looked in. The horse was indeed six years old. Tanner stepped back and wiped his hands on his trousers as he said, "Walk him down the runway, Mr. Teale, and turn him sharp both ways."

The paunchy man laughed around his dead cigar. "He's sound, Mr. Tanner." He walked the horse, turning him abruptly to the left, then to the right. "Sound as new money, Mr. Tanner. You didn't see no flinch, did you? He's gentle, and easy to catch." Teale led the horse back and squinted at Tanner. "But I figure you wouldn't want him. In this country, y'see, a sound, honest using horse like this one . . . well, what you got tied out front?"

They trooped up front, and Jake Teale shoved his fists deep into his pockets as he walked around and around the saddled horses standing there. Possibly neither Tanner nor his riders realized why that big lamp was on the barn front; Jake Teale had been caught bad a few times over the years trading horses by moonlight.

He pursed his lips, sucked air, and pushed both hands deeper into his pockets until Frank thought his soiled old baggy britches would fall, then shuffled back by Tanner and said, "Is that your mark, Mr. Tanner? What is it, Rafter T?"

It was. "Yeah. Rafter T. I ranch up north quite a distance.

Teale nodded. "Sure. . . . Well, they're rode down and all, but they got good age to 'em and all. Come back down inside and I'll roust you up some more besides the big sorrel, and we'll whittle the stick a little. . . . I'll need bills of sale, Mr. Tanner."

"You'll get them, Mr. Teale."

It took an hour and a half, but finally Tanner returned to the harness room with Jake Teale to write bills of sale and to pay the difference in cash. Those poker players had not left the table. They watched Tanner all the while. When he took back bills of sale from Teale and hauled out a packet of greenbacks from which to pony up the difference, they seemed scarcely to be breathing. Tanner ignored them, nodded, shook Jake Teale's hand, and walked out into the runway where his riders were hauling outfits inside and hoisting them into place on the fresh, new horses.

But they did not mount up inside; they led the strange horses out back before swinging up. Only one—a *grulla* with his ears set so close together they seemed to come out of the same place—offered any trouble, and Frank Morrison had that one. Frank cursed, eased up the cinch, turned the animal twice, then swung up. Before the *grulla* could decide on a course of action, Frank goaded him ahead, then set him up and spun his back. The horse forgot whatever he'd had in mind, and when the others were astride, Frank spun him again and led off westerly from Tomkinsville through the bitterest cold of the night.

Back in the runway, the poker players craned to watch as the four strangers rode away, and Jake turned to his night man. "Arlo, go roust up the sheriff. Sure as gawd made green apples, there's prices on them fellers. Go on—*damn it, Arlo, go on!*"

The *grulla* settled down a mile west of town, and Frank surmised that he was one of those spoiled animals that did not make trouble as long as he was with other horses.

One of the range men made a little laugh and said,

"Frank, that son of a bitch will pack you sixty miles just so's when you're tired and get off he can catch you off guard and kick the head off your shoulders."

Frank turned toward Tanner. "Did you ask old 'possum-belly back there about horse thieves?"

Tanner had. "He said there's nothing but cow outfits over here, no loose stock worth mentionin' this time of year, and none under fence except in his horse pasture about seven miles east of town." Tanner was taking the measure of his big sorrel as he spoke. "He said they hadn't lost any horses to thieves in years, and that they got a mean bastard for a sheriff who'd never let up if horse thieves came into his country." Tanner looked at Morrison. "If the In'ians was over here earlier and got horses out of someone's shed, Frank, I'd say no one knows anything about it yet. . . . Angle a little more southerly. . . . If they wasn't here, at least this time we'll have a little edge—we got good horses under us again. At least we'll be a lot closer now than we have been up to now."

Frank eased out the pig-eyed blue horse a little, then booted him over into a lope. The *grulla* went willingly. A couple of the men who had been watching, ready to laugh when the horse fired, were disappointed. It had been a long night and they would have welcomed a little diversion.

Tired and chilled though the men were, there was now strong, willing horseflesh under them, and that at least lifted their spirits a little, because it meant they might shortly be able to get the damned business over with. They chewed jerky while covering a number of miles, saw forested, broken country on ahead, and followed Frank's lead as he turned off a little to their left, aiming for a half-bald hill about two miles on.

There was some brush atop that hill, but only about six or eight trees, otherwise it was grassy and softly rounded.

They slackened to a walk at the base and rested twice before reaching the top. It took almost an hour to get up there. They could have done it in less time, but they had just acquired those horses and the surest way to lose them would be to charge up and halt their panting mounts in the face of the cold predawn air. There was no better way on earth to chest-founder a horse.

Tanner looked up. There was a broadening wide strip of dawn light in the east, far behind them. He scratched a stubbly cheek and looked ahead. "Daylight's on the way," he said to no one in particular.

From the hilltop they could see for miles in all directions. One of the men grunted, leaned to rap Frank's arm, and pointed. A pencil-thin strand of smoke, just barely visible in the poor light, was rising through dense treetops a fair distance northward and well back into the timber.

Tanner had both gloved hands resting on the saddlehorn when he said, "All right. If it's not them. . . ." He shrugged without finishing and eased the big sorrel down the far side of the crest, aiming toward the blackness of the closely spaced big trees dead ahead, which flowed north and south across the open territory they had to cross to reach the forest.

This time they pushed the new horses in order to be off the open range before the visibility got much better, and after reaching the trees they halted back beyond the first few tiers of timber and swung off so the horses could pick a little grass in a small deer meadow while they sprung the stiffness out of their legs and had a smoke. After many days on this manhunt, they had a collective feeling that the end was getting closer. Sal came back from a tour off by himself to say that there was a creek back upon the far side of the meadow.

When they remounted, Tanner and Frank discussed the possibility of the Indians coming toward them down the creek, and they decided to split up, half the men on the west side, the other half with Tanner on the east side of the creek.

The rider who remained with Frank was Lewis Brown, one of the older hands. When they were out of Tanner's earshot, Lew removed his gloves to blow on cold hands and said, "If this ain't those damned In'ians, Frank, and he turns south again, he can pay me off. I don't mind riding, nor even being half-froze most of the time—not even gettin' soaked and all—but except for a decent meal back at the homestead, I been hungry ever since we left home, and by gawd I had enough of that."

Frank did not respond. He was beginning to wonder how far they had ridden, and according to his estimate, from that half-bald hilltop the smoke they had seen had been maybe a couple of miles northward, and about another mile or more through the timber. They had angled on their lope across open country and were now better than a mile north of where they had entered the forest. Whoever was in that camp they had sighted could not be very far off.

He finally said, "If they're lyin' in camp trying to keep warm, fine, but if they're maybe on their way south again, they're goin' to be riding toward us."

The cold morning was brightening a little at a time. Across the creek Tanner raised an arm, turned in among some second-growth firs where there had been a lightning strike perhaps forty or fifty years earlier, and swung to the ground. The four men sought hiding places before tethering their animals, then Tanner and his companion crossed to Frank's side of the creek.

Tanner said, "The smoke's gone. It petered out about the time the sky brightened. Maybe it's trappers or pot hunters —or maybe it's broncos who cooked early when it was dark and doused the fire as soon as it got a little lighter." Tanner grounded his Winchester. "Frank . . . ?"

Morrison was preoccupied, gazing through the cold gloom of the forest. "There is one thing In'ians are real good at. . . . We better fan out, within sight of each other, then set down and wait, and not so much as bat an eyelash—they can detect the faintest damned movement, even in this kind of poor light. They can outskulk us, but we're a lot better at setting up ambushes.''

A rider said, ''An' suppose they don't come down this way, Frank? Hell, for all we know, they could turn off westward, keep goin' through the trees.''

Another rider scoffed. ''What are you talkin' about? You seen those mountains to the west. Not on worn-out horses.''

Tanner ended the gabbing. ''Be quiet and find good cover. Don't get impatient.''

Lew Brown muttered. ''I'm not impatient, Will, but I'm as hungry as a bitch wolf.''

Tanner gazed at the unhappy rider. ''Go get a tin of sardines out of my near-side saddle pocket.''

The other men faced Tanner, and he gave his head a doleful shake. ''That's all I got, just one tin. Maybe the broncos will have something along. . . . Now we got to scatter and be quiet—and for Chris'sake, if it's them, don't get itchy or you'll spook the bastards and we'll have to start all over again.''

''Not me,'' muttered Lew. He did not go after the tinned sardines. If there was only enough for one man, he'd be damned before he'd sit there eating them in front of the others.

It was damp and gloomy among the huge, unkempt trees. Beyond, clearly visible to the range riders, sunlight was beginning to warm and brighten the open range country back in the direction of Tomkinsville.

Within another hour or so, the saloon keeper over there would be firing up the woodbox under his griddle and mashing boiled spuds, cooking them to a golden brown, and he would most likely be laying on some breakfast steaks and setting his coffeepot on the stove to boil.

Lew found his place of concealment, got settled in, and became as motionless as a rock, and just as mottled by the weak, splotchy light. His eyes glowed with the bitterness and rebellion that kept him going. Right now, Lew Brown was as dangerous as a rattlesnake.

CHAPTER 7

The Ambush

It seemed like a long wait, and not even Tanner was convinced they were doing the correct thing, sitting there in the hush and chill listening to their stomachs growling. For the last couple of days, he had been influenced by the taciturnity of his riders. Despite his determination to put an end once and for all to this kind of rustling by reservation jumpers, he was well aware of how the riders felt. Their attitude made it clear that they were not at all satisfied that chasing cattle thieves miles south of where they belonged and wasting all this time, was as important as being on the ranch doing the work which needed doing this time of year so that things would be ready for winter when it arrived.

And now, the longer he squatted there, the more he thought it was likely he had made another mistake. Maybe the damned Indians were not back up through the timber; or, if they had been, and had seen or heard riders nearby, by now they would have struck camp and headed up and around the ambushers, come back down to flat country, and—while Tanner was squatting there cold, hungry, and demoralized—they would be loping steadily southward,

55

forcing Tanner to lose the gains he and his men had made.

Frank Lewis leaned over to murmur his doubts to Frank Morrison. "They've had enough time to crawl down here on their hands and knees."

Tanner heard that and leaned on his gun. Visibility was excellent back out across the open country, in the direction of Tomkinsville, but in the timber nothing changed the constant gloominess. It would probably remain pretty much the same back in the big timber throughout the day. The trees were close and huge, and their high, spiky tops formed a web of interwoven limbs and needles.

Sal, who was crouching a short distance from Tanner made a faint hissing sound, and when the others turned, he merely jutted his chin to indicate an area ahead and slightly to their right. The sounds he had detected did not become audible to the other men for another minute or so.

Riders were coming down the creek bank. Horse's hooves made a soft sucking sound in the spongy earth. If the Indians had stayed away from the creek, up where layers of pine needles on hard earth would have muffled sounds, they probably would not have been detected—at least not so soon.

Tanner looked around. Frank Morrison and Lew Brown were easing down their upright saddle guns, slowly and silently. They did not look at Tanner but concentrated instead on the sounds, which, while increasingly audible, still seemed to be a fair distance to the north.

A long manhunt was about to terminate beside a nameless little creek a half mile or so west of the open country, against a ruggedly rising timbered hillside where the ambushers tensely waited, without knowing the name of that westerly mountain, the little creek, or even the area they were squatting in.

And the range men would have no regrets about the conclusion of this affair. They had lost weight, had been rain-soaked and half-frozen; they smelled like a pack of cub bears, had itchy heads, and were resentful. They were going to capture or kill two bronco Indians, but even that probably wouldn't cool their anger.

Tanner saw vague movement and settled closer against a protective shaggy tree. He could see Frank and Lew Brown easing back a little toward better cover. The young range men nearest to Tanner was flat out and belly down, his hat tipped forward even though there was no reflected sunlight. He had his Winchester in the crook of his shoulder and snugged back. Inexperienced or not at this sort of thing, he knew what to do and was ready to do it.

The Indians were plodding along on their weary animals. They had missed their best opportunity; they had not gone over to Tomkinsville to steal fresh horses, perhaps because they were even more worn down than their horses were and had no idea their pursuers could be ahead of them. They had made a camp the night before and had slept like dead men. Even now, after eight hours of sleep, they neither looked nor felt refreshed.

Tanner watched their moving silhouettes, and his conscience stirred. This was going to be like shooting fish in a rain barrel. He twisted his head and saw Frank Morrison staring at the unsuspecting Indians with a blank face.

The dogged horses continued to walk ahead. They probably would have detected rank man-smell if there had been a breath of air stirring.

Tanner let his breath out slowly. He was a lifelong horseman, and right now he felt sorry for those hip-hung horses. For a long time they had been obeying their riders on heart alone. Hell, even if this turned into a horse race, those two reservation jumpers didn't have the chance of a snort in a windstorm.

Tanner cocked his carbine and found a hand rest against

the rough bark of his tree. The Indians were dogging it along, easily within Winchester range.

Then Lew Brown spoke sharply and gutturally from just behind Frank. The Indians jerked upright as though they had been struck, hauling back to a sudden halt. They were stunned, but that would only last a moment. Lew spoke to them again, this time in English. "Four guns covering you—slide off and keep your hands in plain sight!"

Tanner was ready to fire, his finger curled back inside the trigger guard. He didn't even think about Lewis Brown exercising a boss's prerogative; he just watched the stone-still bucks sitting astride their tucked-up horses.

Lew snarled again, this time in that guttural tone, and brusquely. A moment later Tanner also spoke, and each time a voice sounded from hiding, the Indians moved their heads. The longer they sat there, the less likelihood there was that they would fight or try to run past.

Sal was the only range rider who kept silent except for that younger man closest to Tanner, but he was the most dangerous—totally still, his gun aimed, finger on the trigger, ready and willing to kill. The slightest wrong movement and he would start firing.

Frank yelled, "Get down! Keep your hands in plain sight and *get down!*"

The lead Indian hunched a little, then slid to the ground. Behind him, the second bronco also dismounted.

Tanner spoke quietly to them. "Move away from the horses."

The Indians obeyed, their lightly bronzed faces expressionless, their quick black eyes seeking the bodies of the voices around them.

Tanner stood up, cocked carbine in both hands as he moved into sight. The Indians saw him instantly. As the other range men also stood up and moved away from cover, both Indians shuffled away from their horses, leaving behind

the booted carbines. They were not going to make a fight of
it. They had no chance at all.

The last of the range men to appear in full view was Sal.
As he shoved out into plain sight, he growled an earthy word
of absolute disgust. He had expected to shoot an Indian.
Two Indians if he could. He looked over to where Lew
Brown was standing; Lew was the one who had called out,
the one who had given the redskins a chance.

Moments passed as the men gazed at one another, and
when Tanner finally wagged his cocked carbine and said,
"Sit down," the Indians faced him without offering to bend
a knee. They were wearing holstered six-guns, and while it
would have been fatal to reach for one, there were plenty of
stories about Indians attempting to do exactly that under
similar circumstances.

They knew what range men did to cattle thieves, regardless of the color of their skins.

Lew Brown watched their faces, felt their moods, and did
not give them a chance. Again, he snarled bitterly at them in
their own language.

Both Indians sank to the ground and, without looking at
any of their captors, obeyed the rest of Lew Brown's com-
mand; they pulled out their hand guns and flung them aside.

For a while Tanner neither spoke nor moved. He needed a
little time to get back down from the high plateau of tension.
Then he walked ahead with his carbine in one hand, kicked
the abandoned six-guns farther away, threw a look of contempt at the pair of stone-faced 'breeds, and continued on
over to unsaddle and hobble the gaunt horses. The other
men said nothing and did not take their eyes off the captives
until Tanner had finished. Then Frank Morrison went after
the Indian six-guns, while Lew and Sal rummaged through
saddlebags. There was food—not much, but anything was
better than pine needles. Frank asked what Lew had said to
the Indians, and Lew answered around a mouthful of greasy

cooked meat, "That we had the old man, and that unless they did exactly what we said, we would hang them down here, then ride back up to the homesteaders' place and hang the old man."

It was an awkward time. Lew and Sal were wolfing down food, and Frank Morrison was gazing dispassionately at their prisoners. It had been a hell of a bad, long trail, and now that it had ended, he was looking at what all the hardship had been about: two gawddamned worn-out buck Indians in filthy clothing, riding half-dead horses.

Sal brought Tanner a shriveled piece of what appeared to be the cooked backstrap of a large sagehen. He took it and started eating.

Frank came over and quietly said, "If we get this over with, we could just about make it back to the homestead by midnight."

Tanner chewed, gazing past Frank at the motionless, squatting Indians. "All right," he said. "But let's finish eating first."

Lew Brown was still gorging himself. Tanner sent Sal back to bring the horses on up. Indians did not carry lariats, and there could be no hangings without ropes off the saddles of the range riders.

Neither Indian met the eyes of their captors. Full bloods could not have acted more stoically indifferent. Tanner finished eating, wiped both hands down the outer seam of his britches, and walked over to them and knelt. There was not much to say. They had stolen his cattle, he had overtaken them, and no one west of the Missouri River would have wondered about what would happen next.

He asked the Indian nearest him what his name was—and did not get so much as a glance. The bronco sat there staring steadily southward through the trees as though Tanner did not exist.

The other Indian spoke quietly. "His name is Walt. I'm Ben."

"And the old man is your father?"

"Yes. . . . What did you do to him?"

"Left him at the cabin with two range men and the settlers. Why did he come with you?" Tanner wanted to ascertain whether all the stories matched. They did.

"He is alone, except for Walt and me. Last winter was poor hunting. We brought him some food. He can't hunt no more."

Walt, the doggedly silent one, turned a face of hatred toward Tanner and spoke for the first time. "He might as well die with us as starve to death back on the reservation. He is old and crippled and sick. Go back and hang him. When you hang us, he'll die anyway, but slower." The black eyes did not waver. "Get it over with."

Frank Morrison strolled over with Lewis Brown. The Indians ignored Frank and Tanner to stare fixedly at Lew Brown. The one with hatred in his eyes spoke, in his own language, and Brown spat out a prune seed before replying in English. "No, I never worked for no In'ian agency. I learnt the language when I was a button. From my grandmother."

"She was In'ian?"

Lew shook his head. "She was a teacher at an In'ian mission school."

Satisfied, the Indians turned their backs, and that was when the young cowboy came up riding one horse and leading the others. As he swung off, he gestured loosely with his arm. "Riders out yonder, east of that bald hill." Tanner, Lew, and Frank were still facing the Indians. They waited until the rider had returned from tethering the horses to hear the rest. They were not very interested. The young rider said, "I figured they'd be range riders, only we never seen no cattle since we came west of that town back yonder."

Tanner looked around. "How many?"

"Looked like six, maybe seven of them. Hard to be sure so far off, an' they was riding all in a bunch."

"Coming in this direction?"

"Yeah, I'd guess so. The last I seen of them, they was angling toward the bald hill."

Tanner looked at his top hand. "Go see, Frank."

After Morrison had swung up and gone riding off through the trees, Lewis Brown rolled and lit a cigarette. He was still hungry, but there had been enough prairie chicken to take most of the pleats out of his belly. He was less irritable as he said, "If it's range men, we might just as well let them get on by—for a long way—before we get on with this business."

Anything as obvious as that did not require an answer. Tanner walked back over to the Indians and sat down facing them. There could be no lynching for perhaps another half hour, and he wanted some answers.

"Didn't you figure the men who ran those cattle would be after you?"

As before, Walt acted blind and deaf. Ben said, "We took the chance."

"That was't very smart."

Ben considered Tanner through a long period of silence. then replied, "It ain't being smart or dumb, it's being hungry. Sitting inside with a little fire, wind blowing like hell outside, over a foot of snow, and hungry."

"That old man and you two couldn't have eaten all those cattle in fifty years."

"Lots of starving In'ians. Young ones, old ones."

Lew Brown sauntered up, heard the last of this discussion, and said, "The agency feeds 'em."

Both Indians raised their eyes to Brown, not with expressions of personal malice, but rather with a blend of despair and frustration. Neither of them spoke until Tanner prodded them by saying, "I've sold beef to the agency to feed you people, an' I've seen 'em parcel it out on ration day."

Walt turned his head, unwilling to have anything more to do with this conversation, but Ben answered Tanner bitterly. "You know how many In'ians are up there? You know how many cattle are hacked with axes by the Agency men and hung on corral posts for In'ians to take down an' haul off?"

Tanner had ranched along the reservation border for years, but he had never penetrated it to any great depth; he only went in search of strays, which he had taken back off Indian land. He had been to the agency headquarters a number of times—to deliver cattle, to arrange to buy cut and split cedar posts, and to get paid for his beef, but he'd had almost nothing to do with the Indians. He knew some of the agency men fairly well, had done business with them. He did not know the chief administrator at all.

Lew Brown spat out another prune pit and ran his tongue around the inside of his mouth as he stared dispassionately at the captives. As a youngster he had been around Indians quite a bit. As a stripling youth, he had hunted and chased wild horses with Indians, but that had been a long way east of where he was now. Still, he probably knew more about them than Tanner or the other Rafter T riders.

After satisfying himself that the last of the prunes he had been eating were swallowed and their residue cleaned off his teeth, he said, "Ben, how many times you raided around and stolen cattle?"

There was no reply. Ben did as his brother was doing and looked away. He did not have the experience of older Indians, but he had seen enough; there was no point in talking. Even if they were not going to be hanged, there would still be no point. It was like talking into a badger hole or against the sky.

Lew Brown shrugged and walked away. Tanner, too, gave it up.

Frank came jogging back, swung off, and, with his back to the captives, gave his report to Tanner. "They're ridin' over our tracks—whoever they are—sure as hell."

Lew heard and turned back. Tanner studied his top hand, mildly perplexed. Frank understood their expressions and made a gesture with one arm. "Damned if I know. But they're trackin' us as sure as I'm standing here—and Will, all of them are carrying Winchesters."

Tanner faced the distant open country, dimly discernible through the trees. He started walking down there, and when the other men would have followed, Frank turned toward Sal and pointed toward the sitting Indians, without saying a word.

The cowboy turned reluctantly back and put a sullen glare upon the Indians. They ignored him as they had ignored Lew and Frank and Tanner at one time or another since being captured.

CHAPTER 8

Pursuit

Frank was correct: There were seven of them, and they were following a bearded man who was wearing a new gray hat. He was moving very deliberately toward the area where Tanner had entered the timber, and he was reading the ground as he led the other men.

Tanner spat and said, "That's a posse." Because this had been obvious to the others, they sat their saddles in the protective timber, watching the strangers without speaking, until the youngest man said, "If they're tracking us . . . what in hell for? We ain't broke any laws."

They had been balancing on the edge of breaking the law before the arrival of the strangers, but no one replied to the younger man.

The odds favored the strangers, but Tanner had no intention of being interfered with—by mistake, as he thought—because some range men were on a manhunt, perhaps for rustlers or possibly horse thieves. Whatever they were out here for, it would be awkward meeting them, and it would cause delay, so Tanner said, "Frank, fetch the loose horses. If they want some tracks to follow, we'll give 'em some."

65

They all favored Tanner's decision to evade the strangers, although at least one of them, Lew Brown, mumbled something about it being easier to meet the strangers and convince them they were following the wrong tracks.

They had enough time; it did not take long to strike camp, get the captives astride with lead ropes extending from the bridles of their mounts to the saddlehorns of the Rafter T riders, and then strike out northward. They did not hasten, nor did they make it easy for whoever those men were coming up through the trees behind them.

Tanner rode up the center of the creek for a mile, providing the strangers with enough muddied creek water farther down to puzzle over. It was not an original ruse, nor in this case was it likely to provide safety, because by the time the strangers found the creek, the roiled water passing by would suggest what the Rafter T men had done.

Where Tanner left the creek, he rode almost due west in the direction of that forbidding and darkly timbered mountain they did not know the name of, turning north only when they encountered a fifty-acre field of deadfalls—big trees blown flat in a storm maybe thirty or forty years before. They sashayed in and out for two miles, than came to a landslide of bone-dry tallis, which no horseman in his right mind would cross; it slithered every which way beneath shod hooves.

Tanner made a feint at the mountainside, then picked his way back east very carefully, into the needles again, finally turning due north.

It was not hard riding, and there was no indication of those strangers coming up the back trail, although Tanner was satisfied they would be down there somewhere.

Frank Morrison declined the offer of a chew from Lewis Brown. Frank would have appreciated a smoke, but he did not roll one.

The Indians plodded along obediently. With armed range

men around them, they could not have done otherwise, but Lew said something to them in a tone of approval, to which the surly one replied in English, "What's the difference whether one bunch of whites hangs us or another bunch!"

Lew did not speak to them again.

Tanner would have liked to reach open country, where they could put the new horses to a long lope while the posse was still floundering in the tallis rock, but he only went two-thirds of the way down through the forest—open, sun-bright country on their right—then turned again, still heading north but paralleling the open country. He had developed an idea he liked better than risking a horse race and getting shot at.

He was beginning to feel satisfied that whoever those riders were, they would not be able to overtake his crew.

Now, where they encountered thin stands of timber, they loped. Tanner rode twisted from the waist, looking back. There was no sign of their pursuers. He had given them tracks to follow that were difficult to make any sense from, and that had been his intention.

He hauled down to walk and again turned in the direction of that rugged, westerly, mountain slope. Dead ahead through standing timber, Frank caught a glimpse of another big field of blown-down old trees, but this time the jumble of windfalls was much more extensive and the trees themselves were larger. They were lying atop and across one another, in places higher than the head of a mounted man, and they were so interlaced and tangled that a man on foot would have had difficulty working his way through to the standing trees far beyond where that mountainside loomed darkly. Frank expected Tanner to go around them; a man on horseback would be unable to cross through that area.

Tanner was a few yards in the lead. He stopped to study the sky above this place and the distant standing timber, then dismounted. Lew Brown, having guessed Tanner's purpose, swung off, shaking his head. But when Tanner started climbing over and stumbling around the punky old deadfall logs, Lew and the others, including their prisoners, followed his example.

It was hard going. They got scratched and bruised. A few times their straining horses balked, and quite often someone would fall and curse as they struggled upward. The Indians showed no emotion and said nothing as they tugged at their horses, clambering over what they could scale and working their way around the huge deadfalls, which were too big for horses to jump over. Behind them the youngest cowboy followed along, red in the face and cursing.

It took nearly an hour for them to work their way almost to the middle of the deadfall area, and when Tanner found a decent opening, he stopped and said, "We can tie the animals out of the way."

That took another quarter of an hour, and although there was as yet no sign of their pursuers, none of those who squatted with Tanner amidst the tangle of uprooted dead trees thought that the bearded man in the new gray hat who was leading the posse men would fail to find where the men he was tracking had come up through here, into the downed timber.

Tanner mopped at sweat, then glanced at Sal. "Go back to the horses, and if they even look like they're going to nicker, poke them in the ribs. Keep 'em quiet."

After the younger man had departed and Frank got comfortable against the towering, upended root system of a huge old tree with his carbine leaning beside him, he said, "If they got food, and full canteens, we can keep 'em out for a while, but they can set down and wait us out." Frank thought Tanner would have done better to have kept moving, to have made a horse race out of it. Being boxed up and stationary did not appeal to him at all, not even with a jackstraw jumble of nearly impenetrable deadfall timber all around. They did not know the country; when those posse men appeared, all that man in the new hat had to do was keep Tanner's crew occupied while he sent one of his men back to that town, or some nearby cattle outfit, for a lot more armed riders.

Tanner's head was raised in a listening position when he replied. "We need the rest. So do the horses. After dark we'll work out of here and head north again."

Frank looked skeptically at his employer. It had been almost impossible to get this far through the windfalls in broad daylight; after darkness arrived. . . . He spat, ran a hand across his lips, and one of the Indians, the one called Ben, held up a hand for silence. Then he and his brother rolled over belly-down and crab-crawled to the base of an overlapping pile of tree roots and peered from beneath them.

The surly one growled, "They're coming." A moment later he added, "They're down yonder. I can see 'em coming out of the trees. . . . They stopped."

Tanner let out a long breath. Maybe his gamble had been a mistake. If so, it was not the first time he had been wrong, but that was no consolation.

Around him the men were silent and motionless. Somewhere behind them a scolding bird kept up an angry caterwauling. Otherwise, there was nothing. Tanner finally asked Walt what the strangers were doing. Ben answered. "Nothing. They're settin' down there lookin' up this way and talking."

Lew Brown, sitting like a toadstool, dug out his chewing tobacco. He appeared to be the least concerned of any of them.

The surly Indian said, "They're arguing," and after a pause he spoke again, sounding surprised this time. "There is one with a badge on his shirt." As Ben got down lower and crawled closer to his brother, the surly Indian growled, "Gawddamn sheriff, Ben. It's a real posse." Ben asked if there were soldiers among them, and his brother growled again. "No. You worry too much. Damned soldiers won't know we're gone until next head count at the meat allotment. Maybe three weeks."

The 'breeds fell silent, lying half in shadow, half in sunlight, watching everything the distant riders did, as still as lizards.

Lew Brown shifted his cud, reached under his shirt to scratch, and said, "All's we need now is for those damned horses to whinny."

The other men had been concentrating on what the Indians said, but now this new worry entered their minds, and Tanner said, "If he lets one do it, I'll cut his ears off."

Ben struggled around until he was out from under the towering deadfalls at his back and raised up a little as he beat off crumbly dirt. His shirtfront was dark with sweat, and his bronze face was greasy with it. "They're going back," he said. "I think they figured we got all the way through to the mountain."

Tanner was silent. That was what he had wanted their pursuers to think; that he and his riders were even now up into the standing timber in the distance to the west, where that mountain began its upward sweep.

He had expected the strangers to hesitate before plunging into the almost impassable jumble of rotting trees, where they would have had to drag horses and climb like squirrels, just as Tanner and his men had done.

As he climbed stiffly to his feet, he said, "That horse trader said his sheriff never gave up." A thought struck him, and for a long time he stood there watching the withdrawing posse men in the sunlit distance. Then he looked around at his men and said, "I'll bet you new money that horse trader sure as hell sent that posse after us. No one else knew which way we rode out of that town, in the darkness . . . him, or one of those men he was playing poker with."

It was an idea that required a little fleshing out, so for a while the men sat there considering it, until someone said, "That sonofabitch."

Frank flicked a scurrying little wood tick off the back of his right glove. "He must have thought we were outlaws. . . . They sure stared at us when we rode in out of the night."

Tanner started clambering over trees to get to the horses; it was time to move. As for Jake Teale, Frank had surmised, a band of men arriving at his trading barn on ridden-down horses, armed to the teeth and riding in out of the darkness, would appear to a man like Teale as outlaws. A man like that would think in terms of bounty money. Sure as the good lord had made green grass, that was what had happened.

They had to struggle with their horses for another solid hour to get clear of the deadfall area, and by then they were all sweating, bruised, and evil-tempered. They were also thirsty, so they halted to tank up from canteens. Some of those old dead trees had been fifteen feet in diameter. It did not occur to any of them to speculate about the force and power of the storm that had uprooted them. Only when they found a creek and were watering the horses did anyone remark about those trees. Lew Brown said, "If I never see another deadfall as long as I live, I'll be happy."

Ben led his horse to water and knelt to sluice off a bleeding scratch on the animal's cannon bone. When he had finished, they all swung up. This time both the youngest rider and Lew Brown brought up the rear. They had slack forty-foot lariats tied from their saddlehorns to the bridles on the Indians' horses. When the youngest cowboy went to work rolling a smoke, Frank skived off another sliver from his cut plug.

Walt turned in the saddle and said something in his native tongue to Lew Brown, Lew slouched along for a while looking at the Indian's back with a hard glint to his eyes. Then he called ahead to Tanner. "These bastards are goin' to slow us down."

Tanner turned from the waist. "What did he say?"

"That those posse men will get up north and cut us off. He likes the idea of that happening."

Tanner shifted his attention to the Indians. "They'll have to sprout wings to do that."

Walt looked disgusted. "You're goin' north. That's the way you been goin' all morning. Even a dumb In'ian could figure out you want to get up north somewhere. You think because they quit back there at the dead place they went away? A dumb In'ian knows better'n that, too."

Frank glanced at the reddening face of his employer, then swung his head to scan ahead through the mottled sunlight. In the mild tone of voice he always used when he had a difference of opinion with Tanner, he said, "Good ambush country, Will."

Tanner rode silently along. If their pursuers had indeed gone northward, rather than back to their town, they would have time enough to range far ahead, during the same length of time it had taken the Rafter T men to work their way out of the deadfall patch back yonder.

Tanner considered countermeasures. The best plan now would be to alter course from time to time, to get deeper through the forest in the direction of that forbidding mountain to the west. That would puzzle anyone who might find their tracks and resume the manhunt. They would not, then, be going north.

He altered their route, heading almost due west. The surly Indian looked at his brother and shook his head. Until then they had still been traveling north. Even a dumb Indian would suspect that whatever ruse they might employ from time to time, their true destination was still northward. A string of armed men up ahead, spread out between open country and that mountain, would be able to locate them. Walt muttered to his brother, "Go in the opposite direction. Go south. . . . He's goin' to ride right into them."

Ben said nothing.

They had been riding toward the big mountain long enough for the sun to have shifted position when Tanner, who was out front, glimpsed a big meadow through the shadowy timber and drew rein to sit awhile looking ahead.

Sunlight was brilliant out there, the grass was almost stirrup-high, and birds sang in the surrounding trees. Four large elk, a bull and three cows, were idly grazing. Tanner swung down and walked as far ahead as the final stand of trees. He leaned for a long while studying the clearing, which was about sixty acres in size, more elongated than round.

It was completely serene. If there had been any two-legged creatures lying in wait out there, or over among the fringe of trees, those elk would not be there, nor, in all probability, would the birds.

Still, if there was an ambush, it would be in a clearing like this one. Reluctantly, he returned to his horse and swung up; the damned Indian was right.

He turned and led off southward, explaining briefly why he had decided to alter the course so radically. The Indians listened without looking at any of their captors, and when Lew threw a careless Indian sentence at them, Walt replied curtly in English, "That's all you can do. Then go south. Maybe your horses could outrun 'em in the open, but ours couldn't. They're doin' well to hold up this long." He waved an arm westerly toward the mammoth mountain. "If you went up there, it would be even worse."

Frank Morrison was listening with a stony expression on his face. When the Indian stopped speaking, Frank said, "You talk like an old hand at this runnin' and hidin' business."

He got a bristling reply. "Try being an In'ian sometime."

"Or a cow thief."

"No. Just an In'ian . . . anytime."

Tanner ignored this exchange and kept watch through the trees of the country they were now passing through, down in the direction of the open country that ran for miles between the pair of big jug-shaped mountains to the east and west. It was the same open country they had crossed into the uplands from the direction of Tomkinsville.

Sal, the youngest rider eased up beside Tanner with a suggestion. "We could talk to them. We ain't done nothing. If they got some notion we're renegades, you could show them otherwise."

Tanner turned an exasperated glare upon the cowboy, who wilted a little and allowed his horse to drop back. When he was back as far as Frank's position, Frank said, "Sooner or later we'll talk to them. When we do, they're goin' to want to take our weapons and herd us back to their town and lock us up."

"Hell, Frank, we're not outlaws."

"That's not how it looks to them, right now, is it? We could spend a month in their damned jailhouse catching lice. And I'll give you odds those In'ians would make up some big damned lie to tell them, and make it all the worse for us."

"Frank, one of those In'ians seems like a pretty fair hand."

Morrison tipped down his hat, closed his lips, looked down where Tanner was sifting through shade and shadows, and said no more.

CHAPTER 9

Skunked!

They halted down where it was possible to see open country. Lew Brown glanced over his shoulder at that big, rugged mountain, then glanced out into the sunshine dead ahead. There had never been a choice. They could not have gone all the way back to the mountain, then up its steep slopes, all the way around, then down again north of this glade. They'd have lost at least two horses if they had tried it.

Lew said a fierce word under his breath and leaned to look off to his left. Where that glade came down near open country, there was no more than a thin screen of trees. He shook his head.

Tanner also studied their surroundings, then the faces of his companions, and shrugged powerful shoulders. "It's run for it across the front of the park where it comes out to the range land, or take a chance up that mountain."

They all knew what the choice had to be, but none of them spoke. Frank Morrison loosened the tie-down over his six-gun, reset his hat, evened up his reins, and waited. His horse put its little ears back and looked malevolently around. The other horses had learned not to get very close to the *grulla*.

They knew a biter and kicker when they were with one. So far all the *grulla* had done was lay back its ears, but that was enough.

Tanner shoved loose and rode on a sloppy rein down to the sunshine, then turned, booted his mount up a little, and eventually raised him to a run. The sorrel was one of those free-striding big, sound horses who covered miles easily— and made his rider feel as though he were sitting atop an erupting volcano every yard of the way.

It was now clear why someone had traded him off. He was about the roughest riding animal Tanner had ever straddled, even though he sure could move ahead.

They sped along past the few trees of the glade while watching to their left. If there was to be an ambush, it would be along here somewhere.

The distance was not great if they had to leave the glade and get back into thick timber, but it seemed great to men who expected a fusilade of bullets at any moment.

This was where Frank Morrison's blue horse decided to bog his head. Because Frank was riding on a loose rein, he had no chance to shorten up and prevent the horse from getting its head down. The first jump was high and ahead, and the *grulla* came down stiff-legged. He had succeeded in doing what he had learned over the years; Frank had no warning, and when the horse came down, Frank nearly went off. He had been thinking of something altogether different than this. But he was a sinewy, seasoned horseman and, while fighting to regain his balance, hauled up on the reins as much as he could. The horse went up into the air again and lunged ahead to repeat his performance, and this time Frank was square up in the saddle and roweled him from flank to shoulder. He was mad all the way through. But obviously this had been done before, and instead of frightening the horse, he fought that much harder.

Frank could ride him. He could ride a real bucking horse,

which this one was not, or he would have known better than
to buck dead ahead in a straight line—he would have sun-
fished to the right and left, would have worked his rider loose
that way. Then he would have sucked back, swapped ends,
and got rid of Frank.

Tanner was riding half-twisted around in the saddle,
watching. So were the others, including the pair of Indians.

They had almost reached the timber north of the glade
when the horse dug in behind and sprang like a cat—and a
gunshot from somewhere ahead among the big trees startled
them all.

The *grulla* folded all four legs while still in midair. When
he came down, he landed like that, with all legs folded under
and nothing to take up the shock of landing. He hit so hard
he bounced. Frank, feeling the horse going under him, had
kicked both feet free, and when the horse came down, Frank
left him in arc-shaped dive. He rolled, lost his hat and six-
gun, and jumped up onto his feet as Tanner came in low
with an arm flung out. The nearest Indian was closer and
also threw out an arm. He met Frank's thrusting hand, and
momentum did the rest. Frank came up off the ground to
land behind the Indian's saddle.

Another gunshot sounded, a six-gun this time, with a
louder and deeper muzzle blast. Where that bullet went, no
one had any idea, but each one of them flinched, as men do
who are being shot at—from up close or from a distance.

Far back, the youngest range man was riding with both
reins dangling loose from his upraised left hand as he shouldered his carbine and fired at the dirty wisp of smoke made
by the hand gun. He levered up while his horse was running
and fired off another round, then lowered the weapon,
crouched over, and concentrated on reaching the timber.

They were clear of the glade and into the trees when Tanner hauled back, preparing to swing around and head deeper
through the gloomy forest. Suddenly a lanky man rose from

a clump of underbrush like a gaunt wraith and fired directly at Tanner, who was crouching over the neck of his frightened horse.

The bullet ripped the bead off the cantle less than three inches from Tanner's straining body. Tanner drew and fired, then checked the headlong rush of the big sorrel horse and swung to the opposite side of the animal's neck to fire again.

That time he hit the lanky man. With a spasm of wild movement, the ambusher flung up both arms, his gun went end over end into the underbrush, and he dropped backward to hang across a big, sturdy bush.

The ambushers were on foot, which probably saved the fleeing horsemen. It would require a little time for them to run for their horses and start in pursuit.

Tanner risked a backward look, saw the others following, and, with a wild gesture of the hand holding his six-gun, led them deeper into the sheltering timber. Moments later they were all far enough into the trees to be protected. They did not stop, although the density of the timber forced them to slacken speed.

They continued this way for a short while, until the Indian named Walt called ahead that his horse was stumbling. It had been a ridden-down animal even before it was required to carry double. They all drew rein, and without a word from Tanner, Lew Brown and the surly 'breed turned back to watch for their pursuers.

Frank slid to the ground, winced when he reached it, and spat disgustedly. "That gawddamned horse," he exclaimed. Sal was looking back, holding his carbine balanced across his lap, when he said, "Good riddance. He wasn't no good anyway."

Morrison spared a moment to glare balefully, but Sal did not notice because he was not looking in Frank's direction.

He had acquitted himself better than any of the others, except for Walt, the 'breed who had rescued Frank.

They all swung to the ground, and Walt stood solemnly eyeing his spent horse. If there was further need for flight, Walt would not be able to continue.

Frank Morrison, hatless and without his Colt, was looking at his employer. They could no longer flee, which left them only one alternative. "Go back," Frank said to Tanner. "They had their licks, now we get ours."

They left the horses panting in the shade, took carbines, and followed Tanner, who was sure there would be pursuit, but who also knew that when the tracker showed those posse men where the range riders had gone, the posse men would not be eager to charge into the forest.

They met Lew Brown and Walt. Lew had given his six-gun to the Indian and was left with his carbine. He mumbled something to the Indian, who moved off a short distance through the trees, watching ahead.

Tanner sank down upon the ground, not entirely because he had run down here from where they had left the horses, but also because he did not intend to be a target. The others, including Lew Brown, did the same. The only living thing they could see was Ben. He had his back to them as he dropped to one knee, as motionless as one of the trees that shaded him.

They could hear riders and waited, blending with the speckled gloom. The posse seemed not to have left the trees. Instead of going down to open country where they could have made better time, they were coming through the timber. Evidently having one of their men shot had inspired wariness in the others. Nor were they riding in a group— they were scattered out so that although they made enough noise to be heard, it was difficult to ascertain where each horseman was.

Tanner motioned for his companions to face around. He

thought most of the posse men were soon to be behind them. The men shifted position, and the sounds abruptly stopped. One moment they had clearly heard their pursuers in the gloom, and the next moment there was not a sound.

An alarming thought occurred at about the same time to both Frank and Tanner. If those men continued to try and get around them, they were certainly going to find the horses.

That is exactly what happened. After about ten minutes of silence, an exultant voice called from behind them among the trees. "Unless you got wings, fellers, you ain't goin' no further. You better stand up and keep your hands out front."

Tanner looked slowly around. Even the Indians looked demoralized. Tanner looked elsewhere, then closer. They had sheltering trees, good fighting cover.

Lew Brown spat amber, glanced at Tanner, and shook his head. A moment later another voice called to them from down along the tree fringe above the open country. This posse man was on the other side of them. "Get rid of them weapons. *Hold it!* Don't turn around! Now shed them guns or we start firing!"

They had been flanked. There was no point in trying to guess how many men were up ahead with the horses, or how many were behind, between them and the open country.

Lew leaned to put his carbine on the ground as he said, "Skunked, Frank."

Morrison was still in a very bad mood. He had no gun to discard, so he stood up and, with disdain for the hidden posse men, began beating soil and pine needles off himself.

The same man who had called out before did so again. "Stand up, the lot of you . . . I said, gawddammit, get up onto your feet! And let them gun belts drop. *Move, damn you!*"

Tanner set the example. As the others rose, he looked at

them. Not a word was exchanged as they disarmed themselves.

Within moments they saw a man approaching, moving from tree to tree. He was coming from up where they had left the horses. He was a large man with a thick body, and he held a carbine in both hands as he moved around a large fir tree and halted. It was the same exultant voice they had heard first.

"Stand away from the trees. Go on, move out where we can see all of you. *Get out there!*"

Tanner, no longer armed, stepped into an open space where the big man could see him. Walt was next. Lew and Frank also obeyed. For a while the large man looked on and said nothing, swinging his carbine toward them and easing back the hammer. Finally he said, "All right," in a lower voice, and four men appeared with six-guns in their fists.

Other posse men were approaching from the rear. The sound of their boots over dry fir needles got closer as Tanner finally took his eyes off the large man with the cocked carbine.

No one spoke as the posse men gestured for Tanner's men to get closer to one another. Finally, the big man moved from behind his tree and approached his captives, but he halted back a short distance, still holding the cocked saddle gun. He had a badge on his shirtfront. His coarse face was pocked, and his mouth was wide and thick. His eyes and hair were black, but there was a little graying over his ears.

One of the posse men pointed his gun at Tanner. "That's the son of a bitch, Sheriff. I'd know that killer-lookin' face anywhere."

The sheriff did not take his eyes off Tanner when he said, "All right, Arlo. We got 'em. Now calm down."

Frank was gazing steadily at Arlo, the diffident, skinny night man from Jake Teale's trading barn.

The lawman ordered his companions to gather all the guns

that had been tossed down. Then he put up his own weapon, easing down the hammer and leaning the Winchester against a tree. He seemed to be in no hurry. He pushed both hands into trouser pockets and looked from man to man until his gaze finally settled upon Tanner. "What's your name?" he asked.

"Will Tanner."

"Yeah, I know. That's the name you put on them bills of sale for Mr. Teale. And the reason you done that is because he asked you about that Rafter T brand on them stolen horses you traded him. . . . Mister, you're talking to Black-jack Padgett, not some lousy homesteader." Both big hands came out of Padgett's trouser pockets and balled up into fists. "I want your right name this time . . . I grew up where folks ate renegades like you fellers for breakfast. *What's your name!*"

Tanner had finished his appraisal of Sheriff Padgett before the lawman had finished speaking, and he had an idea of what was going to happen when he repeated his name.

"I told you my name, Sheriff. It's Will Tanner. I ranch up north of here a couple of hundred mile, and if you want to find out if that's true or not—"

The man who had come up without a sound behind Tanner swung his six-gun barrel in a swift downward arc. Tanner fell in a heap.

Sheriff Padgett gazed at the inert bundle of soiled clothing, watched a thin trickle of blood course down Tanner's face, then faced Frank.

Morrison's tawny brown eyes were fixed on the lawman's face. When Padgett said, "I expect your name is Tanner, too," Morrison replied in a very quiet—too quiet—tone of voice, "My name is Frank Morrison. I'm top hand for Will Tanner. . . . Any yellow son of a bitch can hit a man from behind, Sheriff."

Padgett read the signs correctly. He did not move any

closer to Morrison as he said, "It don't have to be from be-hind. . . . I'm goin' to ask your name one more time. If you lie to me, it won't be no one from behind. I'll bust your damned jaw." As he had been speaking, Sheriff Padgett had been taking the measure of the smaller, older man in front of him.

Frank did not speak. He was watching for Padgett's slightest movement. He had battled large men before; a smaller, lighter man had one chance; he had to attack first, hit as hard as he could for as long as he could, and if that didn't bring a big man down, he was going to get a beating.

A nondescript man walked up beside Frank and raised a cocked Colt. "He was fixin' to escape, Sheriff."

Lew Brown spoke thinly. "You better shoot all of us. And even that won't save you. They told you the truth. We all work for Mr. Tanner. He runs a lot of cattle over somethin' like fifty thousand acres north of here maybe a couple of hun-dred miles."

"Sure," sneered the nondescript man with his gun barrel aimed at Frank from a distance of about five feet. "And you fellers always ride hard, and appear in towns after midnight, and pay for new mounts with greenbacks of big denomina-tions. . . . You lyin' bastard, I can smell a renegade a mile away!"

Sheriff Padgett growled at the posse man. "That's enough, Wes. You and Arlo go back and tie Moulton across his horse and we'll start back. . . . That was murder. We'll tack that onto whatever else they're wanted for."

Nothing more was said as the pair of posse men walked away. They put up their weapons and watched indifferently at Frank and Lew Brown went over to remove Tanner's hat and examine his swelling bump. The bleeding had stopped, but the swelling was increasing by the minute. Tanner began to move a little as Lew and Frank held him in a sitting posi-tion.

A posse man walked over toward Padgett, wearing a worried look. "Sheriff, we're shy one. Countin' the blue horse Moulton shot back yonder, there was six horses. Count 'em; there's only five of them fellers."

It was the first time the captives had taken stock, too. They glanced around to see who was missing. The youngest cowboy was there, along with Lew and Frank, Tanner, and Walt, the 'breed Indian.

The missing man was Ben, the surly Indian.

Padgett reddened as he snarled at the posse men, "He's around here. You fellers scour the timber and underbrush. Shoot the son of a bitch on sight. Now scatter out—and be careful!"

CHAPTER 10

Someone's Error

Padgett's town posse men did not make much of a search. Being in the shadows of tall timber—with an armed enemy probably waiting to kill someone—dampened their earlier spirit of triumph. They returned to where the sheriff was waiting and said they wanted to get away from this place, and what the hell—he had all the other captives anyway.

Padgett was willing. He ordered that the captives and their horses were to be kept around the posse men, and led the withdrawal toward open country. Not a word was spoken.

After reaching the grassland, they still maintained that method of withdrawal. They were more than two hundred yards from the timber before they halted, looking back. If the man who had escaped was watching—and not even Tanner doubted that he was—he could not shoot without endangering the captives, including his brother.

It was hot out in the open country. When they halted, the men tipped down their hat brims. Sheriff Padgett walked up to Tanner and said, "You're lucky. You must have a thick skull." He jerked his head to indicate the corpse across a

85

saddle. "Every one of us saw you kill him. That's murder, along with whatever else you're wanted for. I got an idea who you are, but I'll give you a chance. . . . Lie to me this time and we'll hang you before we go back to town."

Tanner did not doubt that Padgett would keep his word, but right at this moment his head ached so much he had difficult concentrating.

The Indian Padgett had not captured was no longer important; they were out of his range, and even if he could have gotten closer, a chance shot might as easily have killed his brother as any of the others.

Tanner knew his answer to Padgett would be important, and yet he could not formulate one. The pain was too intense for him to think clearly, except for very brief periods. He looked at his riders, then put up a hand to shield his watering eyes, and Frank Morrison, who was standing on Tanner's left, suddenly crossed both arms over his chest and said, "Hell, Billy, go ahead and tell him." And before Tanner could speak, Frank faced the lawman and said, "He's Billy Dalton, Sheriff. Me, I'm his cousin Buster Lange, and these other fellers—they been riding with us since Frank James went out to California."

Blackjack Padgett stared at Frank, then at his posse men. Whatever he had thought before Frank spoke—whichever of the numerous notorious outlaws he had thought Tanner might be—he did not say. In fact, he did not utter a word until he slowly swung his gaze back to Tanner again. "I'll be damned," he said quietly. "One of the Daltons." He continued to stare at Tanner for a long time before turning away.

"Somebody's got to pack double." He pointed to Arlo, the trading barn hostler. "You. That's a stout horse. You take Billy Dalton up behind you."

Arlo got white in the face despite the heat. "Jesus, Sheriff!"

Padgett was already taking the reins of his horse from a posse man. He turned to sneer at the frightened, thin man. "We'll ride behind you. . . . What the hell did you and Jake expect, that we'd do all the work and you would get the reward money? Get up there, and take that feller up behind you."

Frank, who was without a horse, took the reins from Tanner. During the process, they exchanged a close look, then Frank swung up astride the big sorrel and Tanner went over to grab Arlo's scrawny arm and climb up behind the cantle. Padgett watched, then kneed up beside Arlo and yanked away the hostler's six-gun. At the look of protest he got, he smiled and said, "I'm keepin' him from taking it and maybe shooting you in the back. Go on, head out and quit worrying."

As they started on an angling course in the direction of the distant town, Tanner looked over his shoulder toward the distant timber. There was nothing to be seen over there but trees and shadows—no movement of any kind. He glanced at the position of the sun, then settled himself into as comfortable a position as he could and squeezed his eyes closed. The pain was not as intense now as it had been, but it was worse than any headache he had ever had.

Padgett came up to ride stirrup to stirrup with Arlo and squint at his prisoner. He said, "What's Frank doing out in California, robbin' gold miners?"

Tanner answered truthfully. "I got no idea."

"They'll get him, like they got Jesse up in Minnesota. . . . Tell me something, Billy—what in hell decided them to go way up there to rob banks?"

Tanner struggled to recall what he had read about the last big raid of the James brothers. It had been in all the newspapers a while back, and he had been as interested as everyone else. His mind was a blank. "New country," he muttered, and raised a hand to wipe water from his eyes. "People know your face when you've raided around the same country for a few years."

Padgett leaned on his saddlehorn, turning this over in his mind. Evidently it satisfied him, because he said, "Why didn't they head west? Places like Minnesota, they got too many people, and law officers, and the army—and the telegraph." Padgett shook his head. "That wasn't smart at all, Billy."

Tanner was holding his blue bandana to his eyes when he replied. "You're right—it wasn't smart. By the time they knew it, they was shot all to hell."

"Was you up there with them?"

"No. . . . No, my cousin and I came out here . . . up in Montana."

Padgett blew out a big, self-satisfied breath. "Then down here, and made your biggest mistake by riding into my town. You ever heard of Blackjack Padgett?"

Tanner finished wiping his eyes. "No." He saw the indignant look he was getting and had enough presence of mind to add a little more. "But I wish I had."

Padgett's expression changed completely. He laughed. Obviously his self-esteem was as big as his large body. He dug in a pocket. "Care for a smoke?"

"No thanks, but I'd sure like a big jolt of whiskey."

Padgett looped both reins at the saddlehorn and removed his gloves to build a cigarette. As he was lighting it, he turned his head. Tanner followed Padgett's example and also looked around,

The posse men were behind Tanner's riders with guns in their laps. Frank and Lew Brown showed nothing in their faces as they gazed up at Tanner. The 'breed's worn-out horse was dragging a little, but since they were poking along at a walk, he was still able to keep up.

The big lawman's harsh voice brought Tanner forward. "How much reward money is out on you boys, Billy?"

Tanner, who did not even know if there was a Billy

Dalton—although he was sure he had read that the James brothers and the Daltons were cousins—answered cautiously. "Damned if I know. I'd guess between Missouri and here it might tote up to maybe a few hundred dollars."

Padgett snorted. "A few thousand's more like it. I wish I could have been in on it up in Minnesota. . . . How about Frank—is he comin' back from California—soon, maybe?"

Tanner could answer that honestly. "I got no idea what Frank might do, Sheriff. Maybe he'll stay out there."

Shadows were forming behind them where the sun was moving lower against a faded-pale summer sky. The forest back there was miles distant now. The Indian on his head-hung horse twisted to look back, and Padgett intercepted the look.

"He's on foot, In'ian. He isn't in no position to help you. . . . Who is he?"

Walt straightened forward in his saddle and neither answered nor looked at Sheriff Padgett. Tanner said, "Only name we knew was Ben."

Padgett was skeptical. "You wouldn't have a man ridin' with you that you didn't know more'n that about him."

The pain was still raging, but now Tanner could concentrate again. "Yes I would," he said. "You could ride with us and call yourself Abe Lincoln and we wouldn't give a damn—as long as you shot when you had to and rode when we all had to . . . as long as you did your share. Ben did all those things."

Padgett changed the subject. "How's come you got a 'breed In'ian along?"

Tanner raised the bandana to his watering eyes again. "I just told you. If he can ride and shoot and hold up his end. . . ."

Padgett said no more but finished his smoke and studied the miles of country on ahead as the afternoon wore along. They had passed the bald hill. The town's rooftops were not yet in sight, but they would be shortly. He spat, scratched his belly, craned around again, then, to kill time, rolled and lit another smoke. Each time he did that, he followed range custom by looping the reins around his saddlehorn in order to have both hands free.

They were still riding side by side, and if it had not been for the men back yonder with guns in their laps, Tanner thought he could have punched Padgett out of the saddle and made a run for it.

But he was not alone, either. And anyway, he could not have covered fifty yards, no matter how big and fast Arlo's horse might be. Nothing on earth with four legs had ever outrun a bullet.

Nevertheless, he was feeling better. There was caked and clotted blood under his hat where the extremely sensitive lump was, and he still had the headache, but it had lost quite a bit of its sharp edge. Now it felt more like one of the occasional hangovers he had.

Farther back, between Tanner and the slouching men with guns in their laps, Lewis Brown said something to Walt in the Indian's tongue, and the Indian responded curtly. Padgett twisted toward them with a black scowl. "You bastards do that again and we'll set you on foot and make you run ahead of us the rest of the way."

They did not do it again.

Padgett looked back a couple more times at Lewis Brown, then faced Tanner. "Is that one an In'ian, too?"

"No."

"He sounds like one."

"His mother taught him. She was a teacher at an In'ian school."

Padgett glowered. "Before I'd let a kid of mine learn anything like that, I'd rawhide him until he couldn't stand alone "

Tanner was stowing the bandana when he gazed at Padgett, deciding that the lawman would do just exactly that.

They finally glimpsed some rooftops, just as the late afternoon gloom was settling. Nightfall at that time of year in the high country would not arrive for a long time yet, so darkness was not going to offer any aid to Tanner and his riders.

They were aiming toward the lower end of Tomkinsville when Blackjack Padgett said, "Tell you what, Billy. I said I'd give you a chance, and I'm a man of my word. You give me a list of the places you've raided an' robbed, and I'll speak to the judge when we hold your hearing. Cooperating with the law usually gets a man some consideration."

Tanner wanly smiled. "That'd depend on the judge, wouldn't it, Sheriff?"

Padgett made a sly wink. "In our territory there's only one circuit rider, Billy. He's due in maybe a week or ten days. Him and me been drinkin' pardners a long time. And I've done him a few favors. . . ."

Tanner was watching the buildings get closer. "Let me think about it," he replied.

Padgett's dark eyes twinkled sardonically. "Sure. You'll have enough time to think, Billy. And I'll give you something else to think about. If you don't cooperate with the law in exchange for my help, some of that scum you ride with will . . . eh?"

Tanner nodded, without looking at the sheriff. He was not paying much attention to the town either. He was thinking that during the course of his existence, he had known many men he did not like. Some he had disliked enough to stay completely away from. Perhaps he may have disliked some of them as much as he disliked Blackjack Padgett, but right now, under these circumstances, he could not think of a one for whom he had felt as much contempt as he felt for his companion.

They came to the west side of Tomkinsville while the wide shadows of a pleasant evening slowly settled over the town. The place was quiet at that time of day; it was suppertime.

When they swung off behind the trading barn, Arlo scurried inside to find his employer. Most of the posse men were tired, dirty, and disinclined to speak among themselves. One of them gave the Indian a punch in the back and ordered him to help lift down the dead man. Another one stepped up in front of Lew Brown and, looking Lew directly in the eyes, said, "You 'breed bastard, if the law don't hang you, the town will, an' if it don't, I'm goin' to lay for you. . . . You won't be the first."

Lew stiffened, but Frank Morrison interrupted what he saw coming with the dry remark, "You won't do anything until you get your share of the bounty money."

The man who had been spoiling for a fight regarded Frank malevolently for a moment, then turned on his heel to go take care of his horse.

Arlo came scurrying back. "Jake ain't in there, Sheriff."

Padgett had demonstrated his contempt for the hostler before, and now he did it again. "All right. Get the saddles off and the horses looked after. And stay here until Jake shows up. Then the both of you stay away from me." He looked at the others. "Give him your reins and herd the prisoners up to the jailhouse with me . . . dammit, Cuff, not up through the front road—up the alleyway." As his tired riders moved toward the prisoners, Padgett added, "I'll make out your pay vouchers in morning. . . . Billy, head out up the alley. Go on, move! You other fellers trail after him. *Walk*. Just *walk!*"

Tanner walked. It was turning shadowy in the alley. There were scattered residences on his left, some with hen houses and milk-cow sheds. On his right were the backs of stores. There was refuse in the alley. A big tan dog with an upswept bony tail came out to sniff, and growled, but one of Padgett's men snarled back and the dog slunk away.

There was a peeling sign over the steel-reinforced door at the rear of the jailhouse. Tanner turned in, then stepped aside and waited until Padgett unlocked the fist-size brass lock, kicked open the door, and jerked a thumb for the prisoners to precede him inside. Only two of the posse men entered, the one called Wes and the one called Cuff. The others evidently felt that their responsibility ended at that steel-reinforced door, and turned away to loosen the scorch in dry throats, and to take the folds out of their empty bellies.

Padgett pointed to some benches along the wall. "Set. Now pull up your britches legs and we'll see how many boot knives and belly guns you got."

They did not have any. Padgett went to a large littered table that evidently served as his desk, flung down his hat, then leaned over it gazing at his prisoners. "Directly, I'll fetch you something to eat from the cafe. Right now, put your hats on the floor and dump everything from your pockets into them." He nodded toward Frank Morrison. "You there, without no hat, put your gatherings on the bench at your side."

As they obeyed, the sheriff leaned against the table with thick arms folded over his chest, watching. When they had finished, he said, "At least tonight you won't have to eat 'possum or bird eggs. Now stand up."

He herded them down into a dank cell room that contained four strap-steel cages, two on each side of a dingy passageway. He locked them in, two in one cell, three in another, then hovered briefly to consider his catch before turning on his heel. When he closed and barred the oak cell-room door leading into his office, their cells got even darker.

Sal sank down on a wall bunk. "I wish you hadn't killed that son of a bitch," he said to Tanner. "I've heard how folks in towns like this one get to drinking, and along about midnight come down to the jailhouse, bust in, and hang prisoners from the rafters."

The Indian moved to one of the cots in the cell he shared with Lew Brown and sat down, relaxed and silent.

"We got one hope," Frank said, "and it's an almighty poor one . . . Walt?"

The 'breed did not respond: he didn't even seem to have heard his name.

Lew Brown spoke dryly. "I don't think we better count on his brother. He not only don't owe us anything, but whatever happens to us, he ain't going to shed a tear. And, even if he wanted to get over here and wanted to help us, he'd be walkin' all night."

Frank replied to that. "Maybe not us, Lew, but his brother's in here with us. If they get likkered up and start talkin' about a lynching bee . . . well, Ben's been around towns."

Tanner addressed the Indian. "You can tell them we're not the Daltons, Walt."

The Indian turned his face in the dusk. "I know that."

"Well?"

"Then what do I tell them? That you were after me and my brother for stealin' cattle? Didn't you look at that sheriff? He hates In'ians. . . . Even if I told him the truth, he wouldn't believe me any more'n he believed you. You only got hit over the head. Me, no matter what I told him, he'd maybe break my jaw, or say I was tryin' to escape and shoot me."

"What will Ben do?"

Walt had evidently been thinking about that quite a bit, because he had the answer on the tip of his tongue. "He can try to help me, or he can go back and lie in wait for whoever you left at that log house, and shoot them, then try to get back up into the mountains with our pa, and hide.''

For a while there was no more talk. Eventually the youngest rider looked through the deepening darkness in Walt's direction. ''Which will he do?''

Walt answered quietly from back in the darkness. ''I don't know. I think maybe I know, but maybe not.''

CHAPTER 11

Thirty Feet of Freedom

Padgett brought tin pails of venison stew and a gallon of black coffee. The prisoners ate like horses, and Padgett returned to his office for a little lantern, which he lighted and hung from a nail in the narrow corridor where it's untrimmed wick gave off little light and billows of smoke.

Later, when he returned for the pails, he said, "There's talk over at the saloon. The feller you boys killed had a lot of friends around town." He stood leering at Tanner. "You've had enough time to think, Billy. You ready to give me that list?"

Tanner had not thought about their earlier conversation since arriving back in Tomkinsville. While he groped for an answer, Padgett made a bleak comment.

"Listen, Billy, we don't have no telegraph in Tomkinsville, but we got good stagecoach connections, so I can write up north for the records on you fellers. I can have them back here in maybe five or six days." Padgett paused, his leer widening. "Anything can happen in this town in five, six days. . . . Fact is, I was thinking of riding back over yonder in the morning to look for that feller who slipped away. It'd

96

be a legitimate reason for the law to be out of town." The sheriff's leer vanished, but the cruelty in his dark eyes was visible even in the sooty light. "This here is a poor community, Billy. They can't afford to give me a deputy. I'm the only lawman, and when I'm gone—maybe all day—I hate to think they'd do it, but then again I'd ought to tell you they've broken in and hanged 'em in the roadway before."

The prisoners gazed out at Sheriff Padgett as motionless and silent as stones. The difficulty was that with a man like Blackjack Padgett—who was certainly a bully, and had demonstrated that he was cruel and had a braggart's conceit—it was never possible to know for a fact that he was not bluffing.

Eventually, Tanner said, "I got no pencil or paper."

Padgett's thick features brightened. Without a word, he turned on his heel and went back up to the office. In his absence, Lew Brown faced Morrison and said, "I think you'd better lend a hand, Frank. This damned mess was your idea."

Padgett returned, handed Tanner paper and a pencil through the steel straps, then hurried back to his office again. He closed and barred the cell-room door. The darkness returned, but now their eyes were used to it.

All but Walt helped Tanner make up a spurious list of outlaw depredations. Frank remembered a few dates and the names of places where there had been outlaw activity up in Wyoming and Montana. He did not believe they should include in their list anything that had happened in Colorado or upper New Mexico. He was leary enough of Padgett to worry about what the sheriff might know. If they made one wrong entry—something Padgett knew about, in which the outlaws had been caught—Padgett would not believe their list.

Lew Brown recalled a few names and dates, too. He agreed with Frank that they should list only areas far enough north, ones that Padgett had probably never even heard of.

It took time, and when they had finished and reread the list, it seemed believable, but Frank still worried. Lew reminded Frank that Tomkinsville had no telegraph facility. That alleviated some of the worry, but Frank reminded Lew that from what he knew of human nature, a man like Blackjack Padgett would never be able to handle being duped; he had too much ego. And if he thought they were making him look like a fool, there was no way of telling what the reaction would be. "But," Frank told Lew Brown, "I wouldn't bet you a plugged *centavo* on the chances of any of us going out of Tomkinsville standing up."

Padgett came for the list and, without a word, took it back to the office with him. While the men in the cells sweated, he brewed himself a cup of coffee, rolled a smoke, and sat down at his desk to read and reread the list. He smiled, drank his coffee, finished his smoke, and went down to bring Tanner back up to the better-lighted office.

He gave Tanner a cup of coffee and motioned him to a bench. Tanner accepted these indications of friendliness and watched Padgett like a hawk, because he was the kind of a man who would give someone a cup of coffee, get him comfortable and relaxed, then shoot him. Padgett's smile did not mean a thing.

Padgett went back to his chair behind the table and sat down, leaned both thick arms on the tabletop, and stared steadily at Tanner for a moment before speaking.

"Billy, they say the James boys and you other fellers cached a lot of loot. There's been stories goin' around for years. I even read some of them in newspapers." Padgett watched Tanner finish the coffee and put the cup aside.

Tanner was slow to speak. He was relieved because Padgett had obviously believed the list, or he would not be reacting this way. But Tanner also had to be very careful, because he did not know very much about the James brothers and the Daltons; Padgett, whose business was to know about famous outlaws, probably knew more, although in a place such as Tomkinsville, where there was very little contact with the world beyond its borders, it was just as possible that Padgett did not know much at all. For Tanner, the dilemma was simply to know how much to pretend he knew.

He looked across the little room as he said, "Sheriff, as far as I know, Frank and Jesse cached some money back in Missouri . . . in some caves not far from their farm."

Padgett nodded. "That'd be the Samuelson place, wouldn't it?'

Tanner shifted in the chair, decided that Padgett knew quite a bit about the James gang—at least, more than Tanner knew—and nodded his head. "Yeah, the Samuelson place. But that's a hell of a distance from here . . . and I'm not plumb certain they did that."

"Who told you about it?"

Tanner looked at his scuffed boot toes. "Frank."

Padgett's eyes brightened. "Then they done it. You know where those caves are?"

As Tanner wagged his head, he could see disappointment spreading over the sheriff's coarse features. For a moment the sheriff continued to lean, then he loosened a little and rocked back in his chair, staring malevolently at Tanner. "You boys, then," he said. "I went over your outfits a while back, including the stuff you put in your hats. There wasn't much money, Billy. No jewelry nor other stuff." The black eyes were fixed on Tanner. "But from this list I'd say you sure as hell picked up a lot of both. Where is it?"

Tanner had anticipated this. So had Frank and the others. They had even discussed it after finishing the list. Padgett had wanted that list for just one reason—to locate the loot from all those robberies.

Tanner met the black eyes with a wry smile. "Sheriff, if we're going to get lynched, what's the difference whether we leave our cache for someone to stumble across fifty years from now—because we sure as hell ain't going to get any good out of it, are we?''

Blackjack continued to stare. For a long while he had nothing to say, and Tanner could see in his eyes that he was sifting through a number of different thoughts. Then Padgett smiled a little and rocked forward to plant powerful arms atop the littered old table again. He made a tepee of his fingertips and said, "What you got in mind, Billy?"

"Five horses saddled and bridled in the back alley, and you across the road at the saloon."

Padgett gently wagged his head. "You couldn't bust out of here, Billy. It's a local boast; no prisoner has ever escaped from the Tomkinsville jail. You know how that'd look for me? There's folks around who don't like me. They'd be after my scalp."

Tanner shrugged broad shoulders and sat in silence without taking his eyes off Blackjack Padgett.

Padgett read his prisoner's attitude perfectly, placed both hands palm down on the tabletop, and sat regarding them for a while. Eventually he said, "That young cowboy in the cells. . . . A man in my business, Billy—and maybe you do the same thing—we sort of sift through and figure which is the weakest of the bunch. We can bust a good set of knuckles on 'em, or maybe let 'em try to escape, haul 'em back, and beat half their guts out. . . . You see what I'm gettin' at?"

Whenever Blackjack Padgett launched into one of these long-winded dissertations, Tanner had time to frame an answer. This time he smiled at Padgett as he gave it. "You can beat him half to death, Sheriff, but he wasn't with us until a few months back. He don't know anything about the cache . . . I'm the only one who knows where it is. They're all good men, but you know how that goes—if a man don't trust people, he won't get shot in the back the way they killed Jesse, will he?"

Padgett arose, refilled his cup from the pot atop the wood-stove, did not offer to do the same for Tanner, and returned to his chair. He ran a hand through his hair and looked steadily at his prisoner. The lines around Padgett's mouth were deeper and the lips were pulled flat. He was furious, but when he spoke it did not show in the words.

"Come on, Billy, this ain't getting us nowhere."

"Five horses rigged for riding and tied out back."

"And. . . ?"

"And—I'll not only draw you a map to the cache, but I'll give you a list of everything that's in it. And tell you something else: I know where Frank cached the money from a train robbery."

"In Missouri?"

Tanner was taking a long chance and he knew it, but he had his reasons; he wanted to keep Padgett's mind on something that might appeal strongly enough to the sheriff's cupidity to prevent him from suspecting Tanner might not have given him a valid map.

"No, in New Mexico. Down close to Raton."

Blackjack's eyes widened a little. "Around Raton? That's not too far. Is that the route Frank used when he come across country aimin' for California?"

Tanner hoped very hard he was being believed. He nodded his head.

Padgett picked up a piece of paper and held it out. "Draw me two maps, Billy," he said, rummaging among the desktop litter for the same stub of a pencil he had given Tanner to make up the bogus list. "How much is in that cache down near Raton?"

"It's not *at* Raton—it's about three miles east."

"All right. How much is in it?"

"I don't rightly know. The newspapers said it was eleven thousand dollars. It was the payroll for some big army post."

Tanner was sweating, and it was no longer hot. He laboriously drew two maps, one on each side of the sheet of paper.

He was familiar with the Raton countryside, so he did not fear having Padgett see errors. On the opposite side of the paper, he drew the other map. It was of country he was even more familiar with, because it was of his own ranch in Wyoming. On both maps he showed landmarks, and dotted lines to the nonexistent caches. While he worked, Sheriff Padgett finished one cup of coffee and got another one. He was rolling a smoke when Tanner stepped over and dropped the map on the tabletop. Then he returned to his bench and made a very creditable effort at looking relaxed while he watched Padgett for any sign that he might not believe some part of his lies.

Eventually, Padgett leaned back with smile trickling past his squinted black eyes. "No guns, Billy. Five saddled horses and no guns."

Tanner's stomach was in a knot. He could not have drunk another cup of coffee if Padgett had offered it to him. He affected a little bluster. "What the hell are we supposed to do if we're chased? We got to have weapons, Sheriff."

"No, Billy; all you got to do is ride like hell, get out of my territory and keep riding. You won't need guns; hell, it's dark out, and no one'll know you broke out until morning." Padgett rose, crossed to his back-room door, and opened it. "Come here, Billy. You see that railroad prise-bar in the corner? Use that on the alley door. It'll work—I can't leave the damn door unlocked. It's got to look real authentic. You understand?"

"Yeah. How about the cell-room door?"

"About half the time I don't bar it when I got prisoners —don't even close it, so's I can hear what they're doing."

Padgett returned to the office, took down a copper key ring, removed a large, heavy old key, and placed it atop his table. "Don't drop it. Keep it with you until you're a hunnert miles away, then fling it down some canyon . . . I got another one which I'll put on the ring before I start hollering that you fellers have escaped.''

''They'll wonder how we had a key all the same.''

''Naw. The company that sells the cages uses the same locks on nearly all of them. Anyone can have one of these keys. I'll say you maybe had one taped to your belly, or something. . . . That don't worry me.''

Tanner returned to the bench but did not sit down. He faced Padgett when he said, ''How much time, Sheriff?''

''An hour. It'll take maybe half that long to get the horses saddled and tied out back. Then I got to get over to the saloon—got to have been there a little while. Now come along, I'll lock you back in. You got the key?''

Tanner had the key in his trouser pocket. Padgett did not say another word as he herded Tanner down the dingy corridor and locked him back into his cell. He did not look at the other prisoners either, though they all stared at him. Padgett hurried back to his office, and Tanner listened for the sound of the wood bar being dropped into its hangers to bar the cell-room door from the outside. There was no such sound; Padgett had not barred the door.

Lew Brown was across the narrow corridor leaning on his cell straps. He called over softly, ''What happened?''

Tanner told them in a lowered tone of voice, speaking swiftly. Even the Indian came up to listen at the front of the cell he and Lew Brown shared. When it had all been explained and Tanner was holding up the key, Walt wagged his head and said, ''You can't trust him, Mr. Tanner. Not that man.''

The other men were quiet, perhaps because they were hopeful, as Tanner replied to the Indian. ''I know that, Walt, but getting out of these cells is what's important right now.''

Sal looked at Tanner. ''Maybe we can trust him. Hell, he worked it all out with you, didn't he?''

Tanner pocketed the key as he regarded the cowboy. "I think,' he said softly, "the horses will be tied out in the alley . . . and I also think half the town will be out there, armed to the teeth. If I'm right, if we step out into the alley, they'll kill every damned one of us. Padgett thinks like a snake. He's got the maps; he can't leave anyone alive who knows he's got them. And I'll tell you something else—he's such a greedy son of a bitch he thinks those maps are true ones."

Frank Morrison was leaning on a dark wall, which had initials and dates scratched into it. "Then gettin' out of these cells isn't going to help any," he stated.

Tanner's answer to that was blunt. "It's better than staying in them, Frank. Anything is better than that, especially if the town really is gettin' fired up for a lynching. Padgett told me he was going to ride out yonder looking for Ben in the morning—and leave it up to the town what to do with us after folks see him ride out. Remember that man I shot?"

Frank remained against the wall looking bitter. "We're not going to walk out of this, Will. We got our backs to *four* walls. If there's a way out of this mess I sure don't see it; not dealin' with someone like Padgett."

Up until now, Tanner had not had time enough to think of anything but duping Blackjack Padgett. The fact that he had evidently done it did not particularly elate him. As Frank had implied, they were going to move out of the cell room into the sheriff's office, a distance of about thirty feet. Beyond that, they would probably be unable to leave the building alive. But the alternative was not very good either.

"What about guns?" Lewis Brown asked.

"No guns," replied Tanner. "Like I told you, he agreed to tie the horses out back, but he said no guns."

Frank straightened off the wall. "Will, we're goin' to be raw meat!"

Tanner said, "Frank, there is a rack of rifles, carbines, some shotguns, and even four pistols in his office."

Up front, someone loudly slammed the roadway door. Tanner listened for footsteps to determine whether it was someone entering or leaving. It must have been someone leaving, or someone who had poked his head in looking for Padgett, because within moments the roadside door was slammed again.

Tanner stepped over and tried the key. It worked perfectly. In the gloom he opened the opposite cell door, then walked up to see whether Padgett had barred the cell-room door. He hadn't—the door opened easily and they all walked uneasily into the lighted office. Frank Morrison let out a groan.

The gun rack was empty. It had been cleaned out of every weapon!

Lew Brown and the Indian went over by the table to search, and found nothing. There was not a weapon in the jailhouse.

Tanner moved into the back room, where lamplight from Padgett's desk lamp did not reach, and picked up the thick steel bar. He had the thing poised to smash a hinge when he heard the murmur of two calm voices out in the alley. He lowered the bar, hoping those might be strollers merely passing by.

But the conversation continued, even after a pause, neither growing stronger nor diminishing, as would have been the case if the speakers were walking along.

Frank looked skeptically at Tanner and said, "Will, the son of a bitch hornswaggled you. We're boxed in, and if they enter and find us out of the cells, they can call it an attempt to escape and riddle every one of us."

They returned to the office, silent and grim-faced. For a while Tanner leaned on the table, deep in thought, his eyes indifferently resting on that brass key ring where Padgett had flung it down. With the others watching, he removed the replacement key Padgett had put on the ring and dropped the ring back atop the litter with all the other keys still in place.

Frank turned aside after watching Tanner do this, paused to turn down the lamp before stepping to a barred front window, and leaned there gazing out.

The town was quiet and mostly dark. There was light on the opposite side of the roadway, to the north, up where the saloon was located. Frank wagged his head as he said, "It's too quiet. There isn't even any noise coming from the saloon."

CHAPTER 12

The Townsmen

Tanner had never underestimated Blackjack Padgett, but he had not thought Padgett could possibly have put armed watchers out in the alley so shortly after he'd left the jailhouse. Maybe he *had* underestimated the sheriff. It was anything but a pleasant thought as he considered the faces of his companions.

He said, "We can go back an' look ourselves into the cells and wait for the sheriff to come busting in here with his armed townsmen—or try something else."

Lew Brown said, "What else?"

Tanner waited a moment before replying. "Is that front door locked, Frank?"

Morrison tried it and nodded his head. "Yeah. From out front."

"Then the only way out is through the alley door."

Frank said, "That's no choice at all, Will."

"Maybe—if there are only two of them out there."

Morrison wagged his head. "We're between a rock and a hard place. You said yourself half the damned town'll be out there." He returned to the front window and resumed his

107

watch of the broad, empty moonlit roadway. Without turning, he said, "What do you want with two of those damned cell keys?"

Tanner's answer was little more than a mutter. "I had an idea a while ago, but it's probably not worth much."

Lewis Brown, who had returned to the back room to lean against the heavy door listening, came forward and said, "There's horses out there. I heard them."

Tanner said nothing, and neither did anyone else. That would be as much the bait for tempting them to break out through the back-alley door as the cell-door key had been the bait to get them all out of the cells and up here in the office.

From his window Frank said, "Yeah, there are horses out there—and twenty-five damned shotguns and carbines." Then Frank leaned a little lower and peered intently up the purple-shadowed roadway. For a long time he did not move. Then he twisted to look at the others as he said, "They're coming. Looks like half the town. Padgett's out front. They just came out of the saloon."

Tanner gave a curt order and herded them all back to the cells, locking the doors from the inside. Lew and Walt had their same cell again, Tanner, Frank, and Sal were in the opposite cell. While the others watched, Tanner moved back to the barred high window of the cell, thrust his right arm through, leaned as far as he could, and made a throwing motion. They all heard one of those cell-door keys land on the roof.

The silence was stifling, both inside and out. Usually a drunken mob was noisy. This mob did not make a sound, and that was even more frightening, for it implied something far more threatening than drunken bluster.

Lew Brown's mood was dark, but not as dark as Frank Morrison's. The youngest cowboy's face looked sick-gray in the smoky lamplight.

Out back, someone fiercely rattled the alley door. They

heard the door swing inward under enough impetus to make it strike the wall. Then came the rush of booted feet and the sound of a man's gruff voice, muffled by the heavy cell-room door.

Tanner's eyes were fixed on that door. Padgett had evidently given up waiting for the prisoners to smash the alley door and rush outside. He had now led a charge into the jailhouse, probably expecting to find his prisoners up front in his office. He could have inaugurated the firing if they had been there.

For a while there was silence in the office. Then the prisoners heard an irritable, nasal voice raised in inquiry. "Where are they?"

Moments later they heard men grasping the cell-room door to wrench it open, and the youngest cowboy gripped the steel straps of his cell. "They're goin' to murder us, for Chris'sake, right here in these cages!"

The door was opened, and one man called roughly to another, "Fetch the lamp off the table, Andrew. It's dark down there."

The light did not help much, but it was an improvement over the near-darkness as Sheriff Padgett, six-gun in his grip, led what seemed to be about fifteen men down the narrow little corridor. He halted, staring from one cell to the other, obviously baffled as he looked into the haggard faces of the prisoners he had last seen in these same cells.

A balding, barrel-shaped man, with sleeves above his elbows exposing arms like oak logs, leaned truculently to peer at Frank, Tanner, and the youngest rangeman. He straightened back a little, frowning. "Sheriff, they're still locked up! You said—"

Other men cut across the bald man's words with angry sounds, and the puzzled bald man shoved a long-barreled pistol into his waistband and tapped Padgett's shoulder for attention. He was trying to be noticed and would have spoken, but Tanner spoke first, loudly because of the noise.

He held out his hand, palm up, so that the moving lamplight fell upon it. "You want this key, gents? Your sheriff sold it to me, along with those horses out back."

Silence settled. The townsmen crowded and pushed to look at Tanner's outstretched hand. Deeper in the crowd, back up closer to the office door, someone with a high, squeaky voice, called out, "By gawd, Blackjack, you said in the saloon they was fixin' to escape. . . . I should have known. By gawd, we all should have known. I'm not the only man around here who never trusted—"

"*Shut up!*" roared the barrel-shaped man, and he grabbed Padgett's arm. "How'd he get that key, Sheriff?"

Padgett freed his arm. "How the hell would I know, Mr. Cutler? Likely stole it off the key ring when I was questionin' him up in the office. I don't know how else."

Tanner was looking directly at Padgett. "Like hell. Tell them the truth. You took this key off your ring and gave it to me when I gave you that paper with the two maps on it."

Padgett's face darkened. "You lying son of a bitch!"

"Someone fetch the key ring," shouted Cutler. "Be *quiet*, damn it all. Someone go get that ring of keys."

Sheriff Padgett was deep in the press of bodies and barely had room enough to face Tanner, his features twisted in fury. Cutler turned irritably as the key ring was passed along to him from farther back. He looked at it, sifting through the keys attached to it, then said, "Blackjack, which is the key to these damned cells?"

Padgett grabbed the ring and flipped through the keys. He did that twice, and after a moment slowly raised his eyes. He was having difficulty trying to reason out how the key was missing, since he had put it on the key ring after giving Tanner the original key and the prisoners were still in their cells.

Tanner reached through the straps to brush the bald

man's arm. "This is the key, and if you'll search your lawman you'll find a map on him that I drew."

Cutler took the key and tried it in the cell door. It worked perfectly. He raised perplexed eyes. "Hell, mister, you could have walked out of here."

Tanner shook his head. "No we couldn't have. Padgett had armed men in the alley where he tied those horses. I don't know what story he told you to get all of you down here armed for bear hunting, but it sure as hell was different from the story he told me to get me to draw him those two maps; he was to tie five saddled horses in the alley and keep everyone over in the saloon until we were long gone."

Cutler looked around at the other armed townsmen, then faced Padgett again. "Blackjack?"

Padgett's face was black with anger. "That is the man who killed Moulton. You goin' to believe him over me, for Chris'sake? I warned you up at the saloon they was a dangerous bunch. I showed you fellers that list of the places they robbed. I told you we'd ought to go down there and set up an armed watch, didn't I? Does that sound like I was schemin' something?"

Cutler reached up to scratch, then looked at the silent and motionless men inside each of the little cages, and finally made a herding motion. "Let's go up to the office. I'll be damned if I know what to believe . . . but that feller sure as hell had the key to the cells. . . . Blackjack, tell me something: When we busted in here, I noticed something. How come you emptied the gun rack?"

They were beginning to shove and push their way back in the direction of the office when Padgett answered, "Mr. Cutler, damn it all, I knew they'd try something. That feller who killed Moulton is cousin to the James boys. He's Billy Dalton!"

That bitter-faced older man with the squeaky voice who had accused the sheriff earlier looked back to say, "If they was locked in, how in hell was they goin' to get up to the office to the gun rack?''

A man with black curly hair and a big stickpin in a loosened tie shoved through the cell room into the office and grounded his carbine as he said, ''They had the damned key, Myron. Are you blind? That's how they was goin' to get up here to the gun rack.''

Myron whirled. He was a narrow-faced, unprepossessing man, evidently with a quick temper. He glared, and answered the curly-headed man in an icy tone of voice. ''You're right, Mr. McKenzie, they had a key . . . and where did they get it? Off the sheriff's key ring. You saw for yourself there wasn't no such key on the ring. An' how do you expect they got it off'n that ring, Mr. McKenzie?''

Men were crowding the little room, some entering from the back alley, when Cutler, who was the Tomkinsville blacksmith, interrupted the argument between Myron and Mr. McKenzie. ''Shut up. We can't all talk at once.'' When silence settled, the blacksmith faced Myron. ''You never have liked Sheriff Padgett.''

Myron shot back an angry answer. ''I *knew*. Mr. Cutler, I knew what Padgett was two years back, and I warned you.''

The blacksmith said dryly, ''Yeah. Me an' everyone else who came into the general store. But that's how you felt, and right now that's not what we got to figure out. So shut up, Myron.''

Cutler turned slowly to face Padgett. He made a little gesture with the hand holding the key. ''Put everything from your pockets on the table.'' When Padgett hesitated, the blacksmith looked steadily up at him. ''Blackjack, you ain't goin' out of here no matter what. But you might darned well make Myron out a loudmouth by emptying your pockets.''

Padgett was as tall as the tallest man in the office, and he was more powerfully muscled than any of them. He looked among the troubled faces, considered the waiting blacksmith, and shot a glance over his shoulder, out through the back, where saddled horses were dozing in the darkness of the alley. But the back room was also full of armed men.

The blacksmith spoke with a different, very quiet voice. "Put everything from your pockets on the table. . . . This isn't anythin' I like to do."

Padgett made no move to obey. He fixed an angry stare on the shorter man. "How long have you known me . . . every damned one of you. How many times have I locked up drunk range men so's your womenfolk could walk the road-way in the evenin' without having to worry?"

Cutler looked at the floor, then up again. But Myron was feeling vindicated for never having liked Padgett. He said, "Do like you been told, Sheriff—empty your pockets. I knew all along—I had you figured the first time you come into my store."

Blackjack Padgett reacted to the old man's taunt like a bull—he roared and lunged, caught Myron by the throat, and lifted him off the floor. The older man tried to bleat while he pinwheeled his arms. The blacksmith swung around, dropped one shoulder and fired a sledgehammer blow upward against Padgett's unprotected and contorted jaw.

The sheriff's knees sagged like rubber, and his large, thick body fell sideways, striking several astonished, bug-eyed on-lookers on the way down. There was an exclamation of loud gasps, and one of the townsmen who had been knocked over rose unsteadily, swearing as he massaged a bruised knee.

The blacksmith turned and looked down. Through a long interval of silence, he said nothing, then gestured toward Padgett. "Couple of you fellers take everything out of his pockets."

Myron was scrabbling along the floor with one clawlike hand to his throat. A large, graying man reached down with-out even looking, caught hold of cloth and yanked Myron back up onto his feet, then watched as Sheriff Padgett's pockets were emptied. Myron just stood there wheezing and shaking, making the only noise in the room as he continued his harangue against Padgett, but now in a weak and rasping voice.

"He tried to kill me! He was going to strangle me . . . I been tryin' to warn folks for years. I think he busted somethin' in my gullet, the bastard."

The blacksmith turned on Myron and glared, and when his quavery complaints did not stop, Cutler said, "Shut up! He didn't hurt you, so be quiet!"

One of the men emptying the lawman's pocket said, "Someone loan me a hat." It did not occur to him to use his own.

More men were crowding in from the alley, and the newcomers had endless questions. It was too crowded in the jailhouse and getting noisy again. The blacksmith's irritation increased until he finally said, "Thin out! Clear out of here." He pointed a thick finger at two younger men. "You boys stay, everyone else clear out . . . and someone take those horses back to Teale's barn. *Out!*"

He may not have had that kind of authority, but most of the crowd had seen him knock Sheriff Padgett unconscious, and that had made an impression. Men began shoving toward the alleyway door.

When the office was nearly empty, the blacksmith took the hat holding Padgett's personal effects over to the table. One of the younger men said, "Mr. Cutler, we better tie him. When he wakes up, he's going to be a handful."

With his back to the others, the blacksmith bobbed his head in agreement. He was holding a folded, limp piece of paper in both hands so that the overhead lamplight shone upon it.

Behind him, four men worked at tying Sheriff Padgett at the ankles, the knees, and with both arms behind his back.

When they had finished, a tall, thin man stepped over for the bucket behind the stove, and as he came forward, he jerked his head for the others to stand aside. He upended the bucket on Padgett's head.

The blacksmith turned, leaned on the old table, and watched the feeble struggles as the sheriff began to regain consciousness. Without taking his eyes off Padgett, he fished out that big key from a shirt pocket and held it out. "Andrew, go down and get that feller in the cell who give me this key. Fetch him up here—just him."

The thick, burly younger man who took the key was built exactly like the blacksmith and looked like him, too. They were, in fact, father and son.

There were four men in the jailhouse office after Andrew departed, and one of them, the tall, thin one who had doused Padgett with cold water, said, "Mr. Cutler, Myron was right all along."

The blacksmith growled. "Yeah. And now we got to live with that for the next ten years. Now hoist the sheriff onto a chair." Cutler lowered his eyes to the paper he was holding. Part of his discomfort over all this fuss was that he had been chairman of the town council the year they had appointed Padgett to replace their former lawman, who had died midway through his term of office. He had, in fact, argued in favor of Padgett over three other candidates for the job. It required no particular brilliance to realize what Myron was going to have to say about that from now on.

One of the men moved closer and said, "What's on the paper?"

"It's a map," replied the blacksmith. "There is one on each side." The blacksmith watched Padgett being settled upon a chair and shook his head.

The curious man said, "What's the matter?"

"Nothing, except Myron's going to tell the world I influenced the town council to hire Blackjack."

"Did you?"

Cutler raised his head. "We had four applications—two from cowboys, one from Sam Knight—who hasn't been plumb sober in the nine years I've known him—and one from Blackjack Padgett, who had once been a deputy somewhere down in New Mexico. He was the only one with previous experience."

"So he got hired. What's wrong with that, Mr. Cutler?"

"Nothing. Myron'll make plenty out of it, though."

The younger man snorted. "Everyone around town knows Myron. If I was in your boots, I wouldn't worry."

The conversation ended there, and both men watched the sheriff regain his awareness. Trussed, seated, and soaking wet, he did not look as impressive as he normally seemed. Someone had disarmed him; the pistol was lying atop the table behind the blacksmith.

His jaw was not discolored where the blacksmith struck him, but it was swollen, and by the time he could focus his eyes, he was staring steadily across at the blacksmith. Evidently he had no trouble recalling what had happened and who had hit him.

Cutler let go a long breath as he returned the sheriff's bleak stare. In a bitter voice, the blacksmith said, "You sure repaid me for helping you get the job, Blackjack."

Padgett sputtered. "You sided with Myron. You got a lot of room to talk! You taken sides with those outlaws in the cages. I told you; that one who gave you the key is Billy Dalton, cousin to Jesse and Frank James."

"Did he tell you that?"

Padgett could not remember who had told him that, so he said, "He never denied it. And he told me where Frank cached some money from a payroll robbery. What more proof do you need, for Chris'sake!"

The blacksmith continued to lean on the table with the piece of paper in his hand, steadily eyeing Blackjack Padgett.

They had not been close friends, but they had been friendly, had stood each other to occasional drinks at the saloon, and had killed a little time now and then in general conversation.

What dampened the blacksmith's spirit even more than what he knew Myron was going to be gossiping about from now on was his own misjudgment. He had known Padgett was a braggart and possessed the kind of arrogance many large men possessed when they wore a badge, but Cutler had tolerated these things, assuming they went with the job as much as with the man. But he had thought that was the limit of Padgett's bad nature. He had never considered the possibility that the sheriff would try to deliberately get anyone killed—and certainly not by duping the town into doing it for him.

He straightened up off the table and turned so that he would not have to look at the lawman.

CHAPTER 13

One Day Later

When Tanner entered the room and saw the soggy sheriff tied up in the chair, with a swollen jaw as well as a troubled dullness in his stare, the blacksmith addressed him roughly.

"Is this the map you said you drew for Blackjack?"

Tanner eyed the paper in Cutler's upraised hand. "Yes, that's it."

Cutler lowered his hand. "You want to change your story about Blackjack giving you that key?"

"No. That's exactly what he did. The key and the horses in the alley so we could break out, in exchange for that map."

The blacksmith studied Will Tanner over an interval of silence, then said, "Sit down. You want a smoke?"

Tanner was moving toward a wall bench when he replied. "No thanks."

"A chew?"

Tanner made a rueful smile. "No. I tried it once and was sick all day."

No one else smiled. The blacksmith held out the piece of paper. "What are these maps about?"

"They're about nothing," stated Tanner. "Your sheriff wanted the head money he thought would be on me and my riders. I offered to trade him that map for five horses tied out back and a long head start out of the Tomkinsville country."

Having explained that much, Tanner expanded, explaining everything from the time he and his men had left the Bancroft homestead, but he did not say they had been on a manhunt, nor did he mention the Indians, except to say that Walt was riding with him and that the Indian named Ben was the man who had escaped Padgett's ambush when Blackjack had captured the others. It made a coherent story even with the omissions, and Cutler was a patient listener. He only interrupted once, when Padgett started to swear and make threats, and the blacksmith pointed a thick finger in the lawman's direction and said, "Shut *up!* Andrew, if he opens his mouth again, gag him."

Cutler stood a long while studying the map, then tossed it atop the table and fixed Tanner with a thoughtful look. "You got any way of convincin' us that you really are a cowman up north, and those other fellers work for you?"

"I could prove it," replied Tanner, "if you had a telegraph office. Otherwise, all I have are some receipts that'll be with the stuff Padgett had me put in my hat. But they're not going to help much. I expect you could write up north. I can give you a half dozen addresses of people who know me. But that'll take a week or two, won't it?"

Cutler ignored the question and stood studying Tanner. His attitude was exactly as dispassionate as it had been toward Padgett. The other men in the room, including his son and the sheriff, watched him with expressionless faces. Whatever he did, and however this ended, it was entirely his responsibility. He knew it, and that was what made him consider his decisions very carefully. There was a long silence.

He finally said, "Well, Mr. Tanner, some of this seems to

be true enough, but we don't know about the rest of it. You understand?"

Tanner was beginning to feel better about the blacksmith, and nodded agreement. One thing appeared certain now; no one was going to be shot or lynched.

Then Cutler said, "But the sheriff here—in our area, that's the important thing—it sure looks like he had some idea about letting you fellers escape—or something, anyway."

Tanner said dryly, "Or get us lynched, or get us shot all to hell by his posse of townsmen."

Cutler did not comment. He turned slowly to regard Padgett and reverted to the concern that was evidently uppermost in his mind. "You sure made the town council look bad. Me in particular."

Padgett was looking a couple of inches above the blacksmith's head when he spoke. "I'm going to make you look a hell of a lot worse before I'm through. You're taking the word of a man like Billy Dalton over mine. He's wanted from here to Missouri." Padgett lowered his dark eyes to Cutler's face. "You got one of the James-Dalton gang settin' right there in front of you, and you're favoring him over the law. By gawd, when folks know what you've—"

Cutler spoke across the rising words of anger. "Blackjack, you damned fool, *there is no Billy Dalton*. There's Emmett and Grat, but no Billy Dalton."

As Padgett's eyes remained fixed on him, the blacksmith went on speaking in the same dead-level tone of voice.

"The Daltons aren't cousins to the James boys. That's the Youngers, Blackjack. The Daltons got nothing to do with Frank and Jesse James."

Padgett was not the only stonily silent and surprised man in the office; Will Tanner was also staring at the blacksmith.

Bitterly, the blacksmith said, "Blackjack, why the hell

didn't you read the newspapers?'' Then he turned on Tanner. ''Did you tell him all that crap?''

Tanner reddened. ''My top hand built the story. It sounded factual to me. I remember hearing that the Jameses had cousins who rode with them.''

Cutler was disgusted. ''Sure; the Younger brothers. Not the Daltons.''

''Padgett said something about the Samuelson farm back in Missouri, so I figured he knew what he was talking about. I told him something I remembered reading one time, that there was a story about the Jameses having hid some loot in some caves back there.''

Cutler wagged his head. ''The name is Samuels, not Samuelson. That farm belonged to the mother of Frank and Jesse. Didn't you read in the papers about some fellers throwing a bomb into the house and blowing her arm off?'' It must have been evident to the blacksmith that Tanner had never read of any such incident, because he looked around at his friends, then wagged his head again. ''Mr. Tanner, I'll tell you what I think. You're damned lucky Blackjack didn't know any more about the James boys than you did—don't they get newspapers up where you live?''

Tanner's embarrassment deepened. ''All I know is that it worked. Sure we get newspapers, mister, but if you think running thousands of cattle over about thirty-five square miles of country, not counting free-graze, leaves a man time for sitting around reading newspapers, you've never run cattle.''

The blacksmith regarded Tanner for a moment in silence. ''It's not just the newspapers, Mr. Tanner. I grew up in the same territory as the James boys and the Youngers. I knew 'em a little.'' For a moment the blacksmith considered the men who were looking at him, including Blackjack Padgett, then strode over to the roadway door. It was locked from the outside, so he turned irritably and pointed to the key ring on the table. "Andrew, lope around front and unlock this door, will you?" As his son moved to obey, the blacksmith turned back to face the other men in the room, wearing a pensive expression.

He was about to speak when a key rattled in the door behind him and several male voices sounded out front, the words muted by the closed door. Andrew got the door unlocked and pushed inside, looking over his shoulder. Behind him, pressing close, was a tall army officer and a hard-faced, grizzled sergeant. They both stopped dead still and looked slowly around, from the soaking-wet large man wearing a lawman's badge and trussed like a calf, to the unsmiling blacksmith, and the other men slouched across the room who were returning his stare.

Then the officer said, "I'm looking for a man named William Tanner. Who is in charge here?"

Cutler answered shortly. "My name is Burt Cutler. I'm the blacksmith here in town."

That did not answer the second part of the officer's question, but he seemed willing to start with the blacksmith.

"I'm Captain Bledsoe."

The blacksmith pointed across the room. "That's Tanner—as far as I know anyway. What do you want him for?"

Evidently Captain Bledsoe was a prickly individual, because he said, "I don't *want* him for anything. We just would like to talk to him."

Cutler crossed his arms and glowered. Maybe he had been a soldier and did not like officers, or maybe this particular officer had irritated him. He said, "Talk," and remained rooted where he was.

The officer's color mounted. The hard-faced sergeant eased around to where he could see the blacksmith better. Neither of them spoke until the captain had studied Tanner for a moment. "You are Will Tanner?" he finally asked.

Although Tanner knew some of the officers attached to the

Crow Agency, he did not believe he had ever seen this one before. He nodded. "I'm Will Tanner."

The officer was satisfied. "I'm from the Crow Agency, Mr. Tanner. We found some buried hides with your brand on them. Informers on the reservation told us some Indians had stolen those cattle from you. We also have an Indian outside, a man called Ben. We picked him up by coincidence on our way to Tomkinsville." The captain paused, then added, "Late last night one of our sentries caught this Indian sneaking up toward our horses."

Tanner was interested. "What did he tell you, Captain?"

"Nothing at all, Mr. Tanner. He tried to run, but a man on foot in open country, even at night, is no match for a squad of mounted men. From then until now, he has not said a word, except to tell us his name." This time, when the officer paused, his sergeant leaned to mutter something, and the officer spoke again. "One other thing. There are two of them, supposedly brothers. We have their descriptions. Something was said about a third one, but we could not verify that."

Cutler abruptly said, "Captain, how did you know Mr. Tanner was here?"

The officer replied as though what he said were an unimportant aside; he continued to look across in Tanner's direction, evidently still annoyed about the blacksmith's earlier brusqueness. "Down at the livery barn when we rode into town, some men were talking about an outlaw named Billy Dalton who was up here at the jailhouse under the name of Tanner."

Blackjack Padgett said abruptly, "There's more than one, and they're all right here in this jailhouse—locked in cells."

The captain and his sergeant gazed at Sheriff Padgett without saying a word. It had been evident to them both when they had entered the jailhouse office that they had arrived in the middle of some local dispute. As he gazed at

Padgett, the captain's aloof expression suggested that he did not intend to interfere.

But Padgett misinterpreted the look, or else he had decided to try and set the soldiers against the blacksmith, because he suddenly said, "There's an In'ian in the cells. He was ridin' with this feller who calls himself Tanner."

Cutler reddened but did not look at Padgett. He spoke to the officer. "That part is true. There's an In'ian in the cells. Mr. Tanner's whole riding crew is down there. I sure doubt that any cowman would have an In'ian or anyone else riding for him who had been rustling his cattle."

Bledsoe raised his eyebrows in Tanner's direction. "What about this Indian, Mr. Tanner?"

Tanner had had time to think while the three men were talking, and his reply was short. "The man you're talking about rides for me. He is an In'ian and his name is Walt."

Bledsoe nodded as though he accepted this, then said, "Do you know whether your rider has a brother named Ben?"

Tanner answered woodenly, "I know he has a brother named Ben."

Blackjack Padgett started to say something, and the blacksmith's son struck him in the face with an open palm. At once, both the soldiers reacted, but the blacksmith stopped them. "Captain, you run your army, and we'll run Tomkinsville. Don't butt in."

Bledsoe turned finally to face the blacksmith. He was angry. "If there is no law here, the army will—"

"There's law," snapped the blacksmith. "Right now, I'm it, and these young fellers are my assistants. Captain, if you're still around after supper, we could meet at the saloon and I'll tell you the whole story."

Bledsoe did not seem to relax. "Community affairs are outside my authority, Mr. Cutler, but civilian abuses—"

"There haven't been any abuses yet, Captain," stated the

blacksmith. "Not by us anyway." He paused for a long time, glanced in Tanner's direction, then sighed and went back over to lean on the table. "This is the damnedest mess I was ever mixed up in," he said to the room at large. Then he regarded Tanner stonily for a moment and made a gesture. "You can walk out of here. Captain, you and Mr. Tanner go up to the saloon and talk, or over to the café—no, it'll be locked up for the night now. Well, anyway, go outside somewhere and talk."

Cutler straightened up. He was about the shortest man in the room, and easily broader than any of them, except his son and the grizzled sergeant.

Captain Bledsoe did not respond. Nothing more was said until the blacksmith jerked his head in the direction of the cell-room door and said, "Andrew, take Blackjack along. Lock him in one of the cells."

Two men had to boost Padgett to his feet. One knelt to untie his legs under the gaze of Tanner and the soldiers, then they flanked him on the way down into the cell room.

Bledsoe turned a quizzical eye on the blacksmith. "Was he in a fight?"

Cutler declined to answer.

Tanner rose from the bench and interrupted the officer's train of thought. "I'd like to talk to your prisoner for a few minutes, Captain."

"Why, Mr. Tanner?"

"Well, for one thing, because he didn't steal my cattle. For another, he'll need a horse."

"A horse . . . ?"

"Yes, sir. When my crew is released, Ben can ride back up north with us."

"He's a military prisoner, Mr. Tanner."

"What's he charged with, Captain?"

"I've already explained that—cattle stealing."

"And I just told you he didn't steal those cattle."

The initiative had shifted. Cutler and the other men of Tomkinsville were now onlookers as Tanner and the army officer faced one another across the width of the jailhouse office.

The soldier was unyielding. "Reservation informers told the agency people that those three men did steal cattle from your range and that you came up onto the reservation with your riders and took back as many of the cattle as you could find, then started on the trail of the cattle thieves, heading south. We didn't learn all this for several days, but my orders were to stay on the trail until I located you or those Indians."

Tanner slowly shook his head at the army officer. "Are you saying you tracked us, Captain? I know better. It rained like hell a few days back. There were no tracks left when it quit."

Bledsoe's thin lips lifted a little in a humorless smile. "We didn't track you, Mr. Tanner. We stopped and made inquiries along the way."

"We didn't use the road, Captain."

"Nor did we, Mr. Tanner. Three times we encountered hunters who said they had seen a party of range men passing southward, armed with Winchesters and carrying bedrolls and saddlebags."

Tanner eased his breath out softly. The soldiers had not found the Bancroft place.

At this point, Burt Cutler spoke in a tired voice. "Gents, it's darned late; you can finish your palaver outside. Mr. Tanner, if you're still around in the mornin', I'd like to hear it all again, when a lady's present who can write real good." He nodded gravely at Tanner.

Outside in the warm night, several soldiers were lounging at the hitch rack. Only one man was on a horse. He and Tanner recognized each other at once. Captain Bledsoe leaned toward Tanner. "Is that your rider?"

Tanner nodded. "Mind if I talk to him?"

Bledsoe raised his head. "Untie his hands from the saddlehorn and let him dismount."

Tanner waited until Ben was freed and on the ground, then jerked his head and, under the watchful gaze of the soldiers, took Ben off a short distance and said, "You ride for me and you did not steal my cattle. Do you understand?"

Ben neither spoke nor nodded. He gazed balefully at Tanner for a while, then said, "Where is Walt?"

"In the jailhouse, locked up with the others. They'll be turned loose, but you remember what I just told you— you've been cowboying for me. They asked about you and Walt, and that's what I told them."

The surly Indian flicked a glance in the direction of the soldiers, then back to Tanner. "Somebody told them something, sure as hell. That's why they was after me and Walt."

"Yeah. Informers on the reservation told them you had rustled my beef. But the officer said you would not talk to them, and I told them you and Walt work for me and that you didn't steal any cattle."

"We had the cattle."

"Sure you did. I gave you those cattle to drive to the reservation to tide folks over until the regular meat allotment was made. . . . You and Walt were riding for me. You were part of the Rafter T crew. Do you understand what I'm saying?"

Ben considered Tanner for a long time before barely nodding his head that he understood. Then he said, "Why?"

Tanner's answer was ready. "You were going to fight the posse beside us, and I got some of the cattle back anyway. I didn't know what's been happening on the reservation."

"It's not your worry; they are just In'ians up there."

"I've been hungry a few times," Tanner said dryly.

"Nothing is goin' to change, an' you can't keep on feedin' us."

"Maybe. Right now you remember what you're to say."

"Soldiers won't believe me."

"They'll believe you, because my riders and I, and your brother, will back it up that you've been riding for me."

Ben turned aside as he said, "I don't know why you're doin' this. It ain't goin' to do you any good."

Tanner's reply was curt. "We can't stand here talkin' all night. Now wait here."

Tanner returned to the hitch rack, where the captain was watching him approach. "Is that your rider, Mr. Tanner?"

"Yes, sir. He can bed down in the jailhouse with the rest of us tonight. In the morning we'd like to head north."

The officer's gaze did not waver. "Are you sure this man works for you? What was he doing on foot in the night, skulking around?"

"If you came south down that long meadow, did you see a dead *grulla* horse?"

"We came down the road, Mr. Tanner."

"There's one out there, over across the open country near the timber."

"I see. Why didn't you take the man up behind you?"

"First off, Captain, because we did not know where he was. Secondly, because that outlaw sheriff you saw was after us with an armed posse—the blacksmith, and maybe the sheriff, can explain all that to you in the morning. Anyway, the sheriff thought we were outlaws, and we didn't get much of a chance to explain otherwise."

Captain Bledsoe pulled gloves from beneath his belt and put them on slowly. "Mr. Tanner, there's a lot here I don't understand." He raised his head. "For example, why would you go onto the reservation to drive some of those cattle back if you had given them to the Indians?"

"You ever been a range cattleman, Captain?"

"No."

"I didn't think so. When you cut out a few head, you always get a few who want to straggle along. If you have enough men, you turn them back. If there is only two of you, you do the best you can, and usually it's not enough—the stragglers keep following. So I went up to fetch back those stragglers."

Captain Bledsoe said, "What happened to that lawman in there?"

Tanner shifted his weight. He was tired to the bone. He talked about Blackjack Padgett for a few minutes, then said, "Like you said in there, Captain, it's not the army's business. The town blacksmith can tell you all about it tomorrow, if you want to ask him."

Bledsoe shook his head. "I know where your ranch is, Mr. Tanner. Maybe some day next summer, when the weather is better, I can ride down for a visit and you can explain all this to me."

Tanner smiled. "Be glad to, Captain."

He stood with Ben at the hitch rack watching the soldiers ride slowly back out of Tomkinsville in the direction of the camp they had established, where they had caught Ben.

Tanner shoved back his hat and ran a soiled cuff over his forehead.

Ben said, "Where is my father?"

Tanner answered around a big yawn. "With a little luck, you'll see him by tomorrow night."

"Is he all right?"

"He was when we left him. We took him out of a cave where he was hiding and put him in the house, where the settler woman could look after him."

Tanner turned and regarded the feeble lamplight coming from the jailhouse office. "The luckiest day of your life was when they caught you before you stole one of their horses "

Ben thought about that and finally said, "I ain't had much luck with horses—or cattle—lately."

They entered the jailhouse and closed the door. They had not noticed, but the moon was gone, the stars were not as bright as they had been, and around them the town had bedded down long ago.

CHAPTER 14

Before Daylight

Tanner, his three riders, and the pair of Indians routed out the saloon keeper before sunup and paid him to feed them. The café man, who was dour at his best and downright disagreeable at his worst, did not utter a word. He cooked a big meal and served it. Like everyone else in Tomkinsville, he had heard rumors on top of rumors since Sheriff Padgett had returned to town the previous night. He knew that the six men silently filling their bellies at his counter were in some way involved, and he also saw that they were armed, beard-stubbled, unsmiling, and not talkative. When they left, he was enormously relieved. He had heard that these men were part of some notorious outlaw band, one linked directly to the James brothers themselves.

When they walked into the trading barn, Jake Teale was making coffee in his smelly little office and harness room. When he turned and saw Tanner standing in the doorway, he almost spilled coffee on the old dog sleeping blissfully atop a pile of sweat-stiff saddle blankets.

"Where's Arlo?" said Tanner.

The white-faced horse trader had to shove both hands into

trouser pockets to conceal the shaking. "I guess he ain't come in yet. It's a mite early. Can I do something, or is it Arlo you wanted to see?"

"Arlo," replied Tanner mildly. Several menacing, unshaven faces showed blurrily behind the man in Teale's doorway. "We thought we might hang the son of a bitch from one of your barn balks before we left town."

"Jesus! I ain't seen him yet today. . . . Mister, he didn't mean no harm."

Tanner spoke over his shoulder. "You fellers care for some coffee?"

The men in the dark runway pushed past and crowded into the room. Jake Teale skipped his eyes from face to face. When the two Indians shouldered past him, he stepped back until his legs touched the untidy little table he used for a desk.

Only Frank Morrison filled a graniteware cup with coffee. The others simply stood eyeing the trader. Tanner leaned on the doorjamb. Frank tasted the coffee and spat it out. "How long have those grounds been in the pot, horse trader?"

Jake Teale made a feeble smile. "I'll make a fresh pot."

As he started to move, Frank said, "You don't have that much time," and turned to look for a coiled lariat. He took one off a saddle and dropped the loop, shoved his foot through it to test the rope for strength, then looked at Tanner as though expecting instructions.

Jake Teale fell into a rickety chair. "Gents, you got this all wrong. . . ."

Tanner ignored him. "We need another horse. That *grulla* you sold us—"

"Wait a minute, mister. I didn't know he'd do anything. I just bought him a few days back, an' the feller who sold him to me said—"

"Who said he did anything? He's dead. We need a horse to take his place."

Teale raised an unsteady hand to a cut-down coffee tin he used for an ashtray, picked up a splayed, half-smoked cigar, and put it between his lips. He looked up at Tanner again. "I got exactly what you gents will need. A big, sound young seal-brown gelding. I know this horse; he don't have a single vice." Teale was gaining assurance as he talked. "Mister, my price for the seal-brown is thirty dollars, but because it's you, an' all, I'm goin' to let you have him for what I give for him—eleven dollars."

"Let's go look at him," Tanner said, and moved out of the office door. Teale stood up and almost ran out into the runway, leaving Frank back there holding that rope. Lew Brown shook his head. Frank draped the lariat back across the saddle-swells and followed Sal outside. The last man out of the harness room was Walt. He paused to lean down and scratch the old dog behind the ears, then also moved out into the runway.

Tanner turned at the sound of his name. The other men trooped in Teale's wake toward a stall down near the back-alley exit.

Burt Cutler walked down from the roadway and wrinkled his nose as he approached Tanner. No one had cleaned the stalls, and the barn smelled powerfully of ammonia.

Cutler looked much better than he had looked the previous night. He was scrubbed and shaved and wearing clean clothes. He must have felt better, too, because he smiled as he nodded to Tanner. "Good morning. I just come from the café. That officer and his dog-robber was having breakfast in there. That's something I remember about the army; they get you up before the chickens so you can stand around and wait. The captain asked if you fellers had left town yet."

Tanner's stomach knotted. "Why? What's on his mind?"

Cutler did not respond to the question. "We talked. I told him about all that happened last night before he come into town, and some other things, mostly about Blackjack." The blacksmith's eyes lifted to Tanner's face. "He was more interested in your In'ians."

The knot remained. "What about them?"

"Well, he seems to think, after pondering on it, that for some reason you're protecting them."

From the lower end of the barn, Frank called out, "He'll do, Will."

"All right," Tanner called back. "Saddle him up, and our horses, too."

Cutler watched the men down there for a moment. "You buying a horse from Jake?"

"Yeah. To replace one that feller named Moulton killed when Padgett caught us."

"Well, Mr. Tanner . . . keep an eye on Jake."

Tanner thought of the fright in Teale's face and said, "I don't think he'll do anything clever, Mr. Cutler; we mentioned hanging someone for what he and his hostler did yesterday. Right now he's too scairt to be clever with us. . . . What about the In'ians?"

Cutler was looking down to where the range men were bringing out horses to be rigged out when he replied, "Nothing—just that he figures you're protecting them."

"Does he figure to do something, Mr. Cutler?"

"No. . . . You know anything about army officers, Mr. Tanner? They're all conscious as hell of bein' above other men. Some of them carry it so far, they sometimes get shot in the back. Some are like this one; rub you the wrong way by bein' superior, but they didn't grow up like that, so somewhere deep down they're decent enough. He said he wasn't going to wear himself to a frazzle tryin' to prove your In'ians stole those cattle, because when it come down to a trial, you'd be the only witness, and if you said they didn't steal those cattle, it'd make him look bad."

Cutler swung his attention back to Tanner's face. "It's none of my affair. I told him we got enough trouble here in town not to want to be involved in anything else . . . but you know, I'm curious—did they steal the cattle, Mr. Tanner?''

For a moment, as they looked at one another, Tanner said nothing, then asked mildly, "How is the sheriff this morning, Mr. Cutler?''

The blacksmith, instead of being annoyed, almost smiled. "I guess he's all right. I sent Andrew and another feller over to feed him and let him shave and clean up." Cutler turned back to watching the men who were now rigged out. Teale remained down there with them, almost as though he did not want to approach Tanner for his eleven dollars.

Cutler shoved out a thick hand. "Good luck, Mr. Tanner. . . . I'll tell you somethin' I learned about In'ians a long time ago; they're never goin' to be like us—not the ones as old as you and I, anyway.''

They shook hands, and the blacksmith turned to depart. Jake Teale saw this and rushed forward, perhaps because Cutler was the only other local man in the barn. "Burt," he called out. "Hey, Burt!''

Cutler looked back and halted.

"Burt, I was fixin' to make a fresh pot of coffee.''

The blacksmith started forward again. "I've already had four cups this morning at the café, Jake. See you later.''

Tanner was eyeing the trader and saw him sag as Cutler walked out into the roadway. Tanner caught Teale by the shirt and turned him around. The trader's labored breathing was harder now—he wheezed. Tanner counted out eleven dollars and thrust them into Teale's hand, then turned on his heel and started down to where his riders were leading the saddled animals up toward the front roadway.

Teale was not in sight when they left his barn. He was in the harness room filling a cup half with black coffee and half with corn whiskey from a jug he kept concealed under the blankets where the old dog slept. A slight sound at the doorway made him whirl. Arlo was out there, and Jake beat the air with both arms. "For Chris'sake get out of here! They're goin' to hang you!"

Arlo was gone before Jake had finished gesturing. He turned, picked up the tin cup in a shaking hand, spilled coffee on the old dog, who looked up in surprised annoyance and walked stiffly out of the harness room.

The sun was still somewhere well below the horizon as Tanner and his riders turned their horses once before swinging up. Several men were standing idly out front of the saloon, as motionless as stones. Only one of them moved when Tanner started northward up the road. Old Myron fidgetted with a crude bandage around his throat that smelled powerfully of camphor oil. Nearby, the unpleasant café man scowled. Myron said, "That's what it took—a plumb stranger—to make folks around here see what I been tellin' them for years."

As Tanner and his riders passed by, they nodded, and the men in front of the café nodded back. The only sound was of shod horses moving over dusty hardpan until the horsemen were up past the saloon with only a short distance to cover before they'd reach the Tomkinsville outskirts. Then Myron had something else to say.

"Look at that bunch. . . . If they *had* busted out last night. . . ."

One of the idlers was still watching the range men in the distance when he said, "They couldn't have done a damned thing, Myron—not without guns. One thing you can say for ol' Blackjack: When he sets someone up like he did them fellers, he don't forget anything."

Myron interpreted that as admiration for the sheriff and exploded. The other men listened briefly, then walked away one at a time until only Myron and the saloon man were still standing there. The saloon man waited until the furious tirade was over, then tapped Myron's shoulder. "You got to find someone else to hate, Myron. Padgett'll be a hell of a long time eatin' prison gruel out of a tin dish.'' He turned away, entered his place of business, and blew out a big breath. The day had not started out very well, what with those cattlemen and their redskins rousting him out and all, and therefore he knew for a blessed fact that it was going to continue to be a bad day right up until he locked the doors after dark.

He was probably right, for no sooner had he gone back to his cooking area than Myron walked in behind two big bearded freighters talking a mile a minute about the evil sheriff Tomkinsville had. He followed the freighters to the counter, still talking as they sat down to bang the countertop for coffee.

The saloon keeper came out with two full cups, bristling as he set them down and said to Myron, ''You want somethin' to eat? If you don't, go on up to the church and do your preaching up there!''

One big freighter turned to the other with cocked eyebrows. ''You ever been in Tomkinsville before?''

The second freighter was sipping coffee and only shook his head.

The speaker reached for his cup. ''Nice-lookin' place— but I don't think much of the people.''

CHAPTER 15

A Hot Afternoon

Off to the east, there was a paler streak of gray light hanging above the darker places where an uneven skyline showed. Behind Tanner and his riders, spindrifts of wood smoke were beginning to rise from kitchen stovepipes.

It was chilly, but the riders had coats, and because they had eaten well, the cold did not bother them. Lew Brown slouched along with the Indians, and all three had nothing to say, but up where the youngest cowboy was riding beside Frank, the conversation was lively, at least on the part of the younger man. Frank was feeling out the seal-brown horse and only half-listened. This animal seemed to be a vast improvement over the *grulla*, but for that matter, almost any horse would have been.

Frank had a new hat. It had once belonged to Blackjack Padgett and was too large, but by rolling paper around the inside, beneath the sweatband, it fit well enough. He also had a new gun. He had given a townsman three dollars for it. There was almost no bluing still on it, but the weapon he had lost when the horse was shot out from under him had had no bluing left at all.

138

Up the stage road about three miles, and off to their right, where some cottonwood trees indicated a spring, they saw a smoking campfire. The talkative young cowboy said, "Them soldiers, most likely."

No one cared particularly who was camped over there, so the topic died.

Tanner kept on the roadway for a little more than one more mile, then turned off it westerly toward the country they were familiar with because they had ridden down it from the Bancroft place. By the time the sunlight came, they were back in territory with familiar landmarks, and Frank eased up beside Tanner to say, "You know, with all the questions they asked back there, the one I was sweatin' over and which they never asked was what the hell was we doing down there."

Tanner looked at Frank. "The Daltons aren't related to the James brothers."

Frank had not expected that remark. He squinted at the rising sun, peered up-country, and finally said, "I knew it was someone. . . . The story kept us alive, Will. When Padgett was trying to figure out what to do with us, you sat there like a toad on a rock. Yeah, I know, your head hurt. Somebody had to say something."

In the clear, still air, every word carried back as far as Lew and the Indians. Neither Walt nor Ben showed anything on their faces, but Lew Brown snickered.

They covered another couple of miles before the heat arrived, then shed their outer attire, lashed it atop the blanket rolls aft of the cantle, and enjoyed the sun's warmth.

Frank drifted back to ride with Lew and the Indians. What conversation there had been dwindled down to silence after the pleasant warmth descended, and the riders moved along drowsing in their saddles. Frank considered his companions and addressed Walt, because he'd never got any very satisfactory answers from Ben.

"What was in that medicine bag you fellers gave the homesteader woman?"

"Money. A hunnert dollars in little gold coins."

Frank blinked. "That's a lot of money."

Ben turned on Frank. "What was your pa's life worth?"

Frank checked a sharp retort, waited a moment, then said, "They sure as hell can use it."

"The old man better be alive."

This time Frank did not check his irritation. "If you damned fools hadn't fetched him along. . . . All you got to do is look at him to see he couldn't stand that kind of riding."

Ben rode stonily along in silence, but Walt said, "It's better for a man to die on the trail than settin' by his stone ring with no wood to burn nor any food to eat."

Frank rode for fifty yards without speaking, then said, "Yeah, I guess it is."

Until now Lew Brown had been riding along listening but saying nothing. Now he had a question. "Where did you fellers get a hundred dollars?"

"The old man had it."

"Well, why didn't you buy cattle with it, instead of stealin' them?"

"Because we didn't have no money, and didn't know the old man had any until we had to ride for it and he showed us the bag to get us to take him along—I got no idea how long he'd had it hid away."

Lew looped his reins and went to work rolling a cigarette. For a while there was no more talk among them, not until Frank said, "Walt, what comes next?"

Walt made a sweeping gesture in the direction of the distant sun-bright mountains. "Big country. We're goin' far back, where the people used to live. Make a good camp. Fix up a good brush shelter to live in and where the old man can

keep warm, and live like him and the others used to live . . .
like *men*."

Frank thought about that. "The soldiers'll find you. If
they catch you off the reservation, they'll give you hell."

"They won't find us. No one will find us if we don't want
them to. That's big country. We'll stay to ourselves, hunt,
and keep out of sight."

Ben turned toward Frank. "Unless you tell 'em."

Morrison gazed a long time at Ben. "I'm not going to tell
anyone anything. After you ride off, I never even heard of
you. But you ought to think about something. Those soldiers
who were lookin' for you didn't get that close by reading
your sign. Indian informers on the reservation told them
who you were, what you had done, and which way you had
ridden off."

Ben straightened forward in the saddle and had nothing
more to say. Walt was also silent. Lew and Frank exchanged
a look, then Lew shrugged wide shoulders and slouched
along as he finished his smoke. Frank had to accept the
ensuing silence. He thought he had given the Indians something to worry about, and that had been his exact intention,
because he did not believe it was any longer possible for Indians to become hide-outs; those days, too, were gone.

Tanner swung off for a nooning near a creek. They freed
the horses, pooled what they had in their saddlebags—which
was not very much—and made up the difference with creek
water. They had time to lie back in tree shade while the
horses ate. From beneath the hat that kept sunlight out of his
eyes as he lay stretched out, Lew Brown said, "Will, by my
calculations we been on the trail a month. You know what
we accomplished in that time?"

Tanner knew very well what they had accomplished—
nothing, and they had damn near been killed doing it.
"Yeah, I know," he muttered from where he had been trying to doze before the deerflies had found him.

Lew ignored the tone of Tanner's reply. "Lost a month's work up where we belong. You spent good money for horses and whatnot. We danged near got lynched by some sorry human specimens . . . and we didn't do anything about what we rode our butts off to do."

The youngest cowboy had been listening with his shoulders against a fir tree. He had not had much to say over the past few hours. "I'll tell you what we did," he said. "Come down to figuring that it's not all either right or wrong; it's maybe a little bit of both, and a hell of a lot of something in between. I've never seen a lynchin' in my life and wasn't sure when we caught 'em I could haul on the rope. . . . I'm just thankful I didn't have to find out."

Lew Brown lifted his hat and stared at the young man. No one said any more on the topic of what they had done with their time and resources for the past month.

They would have been content to lie there longer, but by now the deerflies were all around the place. No flies range men encountered could sting like deerflies.

When they were back on the trail with the eastern spine of a rough hill on their left, they knew the place because of the ridge along its top. It was where they'd been when they had been heading southward in the bad weather and had first seen the Bancroft place.

The sun was well along, and the heat had worn out its welcome about the time they had ridden away from the nooning ground.

Lew, riding with the Indians, smiled to himself. They were that much farther north. It was still a considerable distance to the Rafter T home-place, but from here on they would be in familiar territory every mile of the way, and to a man with Lew Brown's temperament, that was important.

Without warning, Ben turned and jutted his jaw in the direction of his brother. "You know what he wears inside his shirt?"

It required a moment for Lew to realize he was being spoken to. "No."

"A cross a nun give him at the mission school."

Lew thought about that for a while. He was a range man—had been one for all of his adult years. When he was a child and his mother had been alive, he'd attended Sunday school back in Council Bluffs. Since then he had been inside a church once, to attend the funeral of a range man who died of a broken neck when a runaway horse had taken him over a low cliff. He shifted in the saddle.

"What's wrong with that?" he asked.

Ben lifted his gaze to the far mountains and did not reply.

Lew lifted his hat to scratch, reset the hat, and cast an exasperated look at Ben. Damned Indians; sometimes they didn't make a lick of sense. He fished around for his tobacco sack. In fact, most times they didn't make a lick of sense!

They sighted the meadow with the log house in the center by a little past midafternoon.

There were heat waves out there, which was not exactly unusual for this late season of the year. It did not necessarily mean it would be the same one day hence; autumn in the high country was the most unpredictable time of year. As they rode, Tanner had been watching some soiled, motionless distant cloud banks that seemed to hang directly above the highest peaks. He was still studying them when Frank rode up beside him and said, "Will, somethin' I don't have figured out—that business with the keys back yonder."

Tanner went right on looking at those cloud banks. When he spoke, it was not to explain anything but simply to say, "Frank, I don't think in all my life I ever told so many lies as I did back there." Then he relented. "When it was clear to me Padgett never expected us to escape, I figured he meant to come in shooting, or to gag us and take us out to be lynched. That key ring was on the table when I was thinking about that. It came to me that sure as hell he'd search me and find that damned key he had given me. He'd show that to the townsmen. He'd say I had the key taped to me someway, that it was a duplicate to the key on his ring up in the office. So I took the key off his ring and flung it atop the jailhouse roof. There wasn't any other way I was going to convince those townsmen that was the key off his ring . . . and I wasn't sure I'd even get the chance to say that much, so as soon as they came into the cell room I started talking. I had to accuse Padgett of lying and make them believe I was telling the truth—which I wasn't—and that's what I meant a minute ago; I never told so many lies one right after the other before in my life."

Morrison rode along with his gaze fixed on the log house. After a while he said, "As long as you're feelin' guilty and all, that In'ian poke on the shelf I told you about—well, it's got a hundred dollars in gold in it the broncos gave to the settler woman to take care of the old man."

Tanner turned in surprise. "Who told you that?"

"The In'ians. They said their pa had it. They didn't know he had the money until they were going to ride for it and he showed it to them."

Tanner straightened forward in the saddle. "You had a reason for telling me that, Frank?"

"Yeah. You don't want any more guilt, do you?"

Tanner snorted. "I wasn't going to lynch them—not after they were in it up to their gullets like the rest of us back in Tomkinsville."

Frank spat cotton to the left. He was thirsty.

CHAPTER 16

Thunderhead Sky

Dutch Meier was standing on the porch watching when they threw him a wave and turned off to care for their animals at the horse shed. He looked shaved and clean and well fed as he walked down to meet them. He jerked his head. "I thought you was goin' to hang those In'ians."

Tanner answered while looping the latigo through his cinch ring. "Well, we didn't."

"I see that. You brought 'em up here to do it?"

Tanner lifted off the saddle. "No. . . . How's the old man?"

"Gettin' better by the day. He's an interestin' old cuss. Been teaching the lad In'ian talk." Dutch stopped speaking for a moment, then said, "Those aren't Rafter T horses."

Lew Brown, who'd finished caring for his horse, said "We traded horses down at Tomkinsville." He wrinkled his nose. "I smell food cooking. I could eat the tail-end off a skunk if someone held its head."

Dutch hesitated a few moments, looking from Frank to Tanner, but they ignored him and went on tending to their animals, so he shrugged and led the way across the yard.

145

Carl, the raw-boned young cowboy was on the porch grinning widely. He, too, was shaved and contented-looking. He watched the men cross toward him and said, "You fellers don't look real good," and got some waspish glares. Then he saw Walt and Ben, and his smile died. But it was clear from the mood of Tanner and his companions that this was no time for questions. He turned as the door at his back swung inward, and the nearly toothless old man came out, followed by the Bancroft boy. Mrs. Bancroft appeared in the doorway and stopped there. She had both hands clasped beneath her apron as she looked from Tanner to the others, then back again to Tanner.

The Indians remained on the porch as everyone else went into the house. Carl said, "Elk rump, fried spuds and herb tea. Miz' Bancroft's been cookin' since morning. She said you'd be along."

Tanner saw the woman looking at him, and smiled. "Probably smelled us," he said. She faintly smiled at him but said nothing about why she had thought they would be back today. Instead she said, "I thought you weren't going to fetch them back, Mr. Tanner."

The aromas of cooking inside the house were very tantalizing. Tanner said, "Things got changed, Miz' Bancroft. . . . Whatever you're cooking sure smells good."

She was not to be put off. "So's you can lynch them here, Mr. Tanner?"

"No ma'am. There's not going to be any hanging. . . . We've been living off creek water and scraps all day."

"That's not my fault, Mr. Tanner." She turned toward the stove. "Set down at the table."

They sat, and the Indians did not come inside, so John went to the door. He looked left and right and finally faced his mother across the room. "Isn't anyone out there. . . . They're gone." He moved clear of the door as though he expected the range men to spring up and burst out of the house. Instead, Tanner looked into the large crockery bowl the woman had placed on the table, and, as though John had not spoken—in fact, as though the youth did not exist—the range men began ladling food onto their plates.

The boy stood by the open door looking bewildered, but his mother probably had sensed a difference in the range men as she watched them trooping toward the house from the horse shed with the Indians walking among them.

She did not believe Tanner wanted to talk about whatever it was that had changed his intentions, so she changed the subject and said, "There is a warm-water creek north a short distance, Mr. Tanner. The day you rode in, John and I had just finished making a batch of new soap. I'd be right pleased to give you two cakes of it."

Tanner reddened and replied without raising his head, "We're obliged, Miz' Bancroft. . . . That bad?"

"That bad," the woman said, and from over by the door her son spoke louder. "Mr. Tanner, the Indians are gone."

Lew Brown spoke between mouthfuls. "You better get a plate, boy; there isn't going to be anything left directly."

The boy looked again at his mother. She coolly returned his look and motioned him away from the door. "Sit down, Son. I'll get you a plate."

Nothing more was said about the Indians. In fact, very little of anything was said until the men were sitting back and the woman brought more herb tea. Then Lew Brown made a short, guttural statement and raised his cup. "That means, 'Always good hunting.' "

That was all.

Later they went down to the shed to make certain the horses had found water and also to pitch each animal another smidgen of hay. Dusk had arrived, and those banks of huge gray-bordered clouds seemed to have moved slightly down-country since the Rafter T men had been eating supper.

Tanner went out back to study the sky, and Frank joined

him, looking up and around, even sniffing a little. "Looks like those In'ians are goin' to get soaked," he said. "And when they get back, someone sure as hell is goin' to tell the agency people they're back again, and that means reservation police and maybe soldiers'll be after them."

Tanner continued to study the sky. He did not believe it would rain, or, if it did, not for another two or three days. "You're not their wet nurse, Frank."

Inside, the others had unrolled their blankets and turned in. Dusk had yielded to soft, still darkness. They were tired and they were full. Tanner and Morrison also bedded down.

This day had not been particularly grueling, but a lot of other things had been, and for the first time in a while they could close their eyes without wondering what was going to awaken them.

Nothing did. They did not even stir when the sun came. Lew and Frank were still sleeping, but Tanner was out back feeding the livestock when Dutch and Carl came noisily down from the house to lend a hand. After they had all rolled up their bedrolls, John came down from the house to announce that his mother had layed out his father's straight razor, a bar of soap, and a steel mirror on the rear porch, and said that she was also heating water.

Frank rose a little stiffly from lashing the bedding to the back of his saddle. "Boy, your ma is a person you got reason to be proud of."

The youth was pleased. "I told you she was the best cook around, Mr. Morrison."

"Yeah . . . well, I meant more'n just her cooking. Don't stand there. Go lend her a hand. We'll be along directly."

Tanner was lashing his bedroll when Dutch Meier said, "I was worried they might run off the horses."

Tanner had nothing to say about that, but as he rose and dusted his knees, he said, "If we leave right after breakfast, we can ride a pretty fair hole in the daylight before nightfall. I'm anxious to get back."

Sal had a comment to make about that. "So's we can get back and work our butts off to make up for all the time we wasted."

Tanner turned, and so did Lew Brown, but Frank intervened by saying dryly, "I wouldn't want to be your age again for a big pile of money. Now come along, I can smell the cooking." But as the other men trooped out of the shed on their way to the porch, Frank grabbed the youngest cowboy's arm and said, "Boy, think how something is goin' to sound before you say it. If you don't learn to do that, someday someone is going to bust your nose." He released his grip and stepped around the younger man on his way to join the others at the porch.

There was a dented basin, a pitcher of hot water, a chunk of brown soap, and a boxed whetstone beside an ivory-handled straight razor on the washboard, above which hung a steel mirror. There was one towel, frayed but clean, which would be adequate for the first two men who used it—that was why someone as wise as God had invented shirttails.

The smell of frying meat drifted out to them. Lew nudged Frank while they were waiting their turns with the razor and said, "Tell you something, partner—it'd be real easy to get used to something like this. Hot water waitin' when you get up in the morning, and food cooking."

Frank, leaning down upon the porch railing, crinkled his eyes and continued to study the sky. His private opinion was that Tanner was wrong—that it was going to rain this very day, not a day or two ahead. He straightened up and turned toward Lew. "You were married once, weren't you?"

Brown's tawny eyes stopped drifting. Yeah . . . but she wasn't like this settler woman. I guess it's easy for a woman to fool a man, when he's young anyway. I didn't learn for ten years after she run off with a traveling hardware peddler that they wasn't all like that.''

Frank Morrison did not like confidences and had not expected one this time. He looked around to where Tanner was drying off and said, ''You're next, Lew.''

Tanner flung away his shaving water, dried the razor, and turned toward the railing as Lew stepped up to pour water into the basin and peer at himself in the mirror. Frank was working on a broken fingernail with his Barlow knife and did not look up as Tanner settled beside him, feeling raw in the face, but a lot cleaner and more presentable.

''Lots to catch up on when we get back,'' Tanner said. ''Bring in the cattle from the foothills . . . pull shoes and turn out the loose stock.''

Frank snapped his knife closed and dropped it into a pocket, and leaned there watching Lew Brown go very gingerly over his face with a razor that was beginning to get dull.

''And stock up on winter grub,'' Tanner said. ''Make a few trips to the mountains with the wagons for winter wood. . . .''

Frank watched Lew trickle a handful of hot water over one raw cheek. When one man had worked for another man, in and out of the saddle, as long as Frank had worked for Tanner, it was not a matter of mind reading; it was simple intuition.

Frank said, ''What are you gettin' at, Will?''

''Those two In'ians.''

''I thought so. What about them?''

''I know I said we weren't their wet nurses, Frank, but hell, it'd only be a day or two out of our way to the agency.''

''Why?''

''To tell 'em we gave those cattle to them.''

Lew Brown swore when he cut his chin, and Tanner ignored that as he said, ''It's only another eighteen or twenty miles, and we could turn back and be on the ranch in plenty of time. Another couple of days isn't going to make or break us.''

Frank was watching Lew pitch away his basinful of water when he said, ''You're the boss, Will.''

Tanner shifted a little on the railing. ''What do you think?''

Frank straightened up because it was finally his turn with the razor. ''Suits me fine,'' he replied, and moved over to the washboard.

John came out to say breakfast was ready, and as all but Frank Morrison pushed inside, a big crow went flapping overhead toward the distant trees. Frank eyed him, then finished shaving. ''Crows,'' he muttered under his breath, and felt his face. It was not smooth, but it was smoother than it had been. He dried the razor and took it inside with him, along with the whetstone which no one had bothered to use.

There was one place left at the table, which he took, and when the woman brought his hot herb tea, she looked a little critically at his face. ''When you get up to the creek, Mr. Morrison, use that soap and you'll be almost as good as new.'' She turned back to the stove, and Frank started eating. Lew was right about that woman; even with her husband gone, she was more than a match for anything destiny or fate—or anyone—might throw at her. But that kind was sure as hell not likely to be common.

Nothing was said during the meal. When they all pushed back, there was nothing left, and that was something else Frank noticed; the woman had some way of knowing exactly how much food to cook.

It was time to ride. As they rose, John and his mother stood by the stove watching them. They were awkward about expressing gratitude, but what they did try to convey was heartfelt. The woman did not help much; she went out onto the porch, hands clasped under her apron, without saying a word.

The last thing Tanner had done before leaving the house was fold a crumpled packet of greenbacks and shove them beneath his empty plate. He knew better than to try and hand her money.

He hung back until his men were partway over to the horse shed. Then he winked at John and gave him a rough pat on the shoulder, and raised his eyes to the woman. "What you wanted to know last night. . . . Yeah, those were the In'ians who stole my cattle. But we ran into trouble down at Tomkinsville—you'll likely hear about it the next time you're down there—and the In'ians stayed right alongside us. There's more, but that's the part that matters, I guess."

"But they did steal the cattle."

"Yes. I guess there is too many In'ians, or not enough beef on the reservation. Anyway, they stole them to feed hungry In'ians. That's not the same as rustling cattle to sell them, is it?"

"No," she said, and, putting her head slightly to one side, she also said, "Are you a married man, Mr. Tanner?"

"No ma'am."

"That's too bad. . . . Come inside, Son."

Tanner walked down to where his men were saddling up. He had never thought it was too bad.

They left the yard riding in the direction of the easterly slope but did not go up it; there was no longer any reason to ride high ground in order to be able to see miles ahead.

An hour later they came upon the warm-water creek the woman had mentioned, but they did not stop. There would be time to sluice off, maybe tomorrow or the next day—and besides, being out of doors was not the same as sitting around inside a house where a fire was burning.

They were passing through some burnished, leathery-red

autumn underbrush when Carl said, "When you got down to that town, didn't the law help you?"

Lew Brown replied with a perfectly straight face. "Help us? By golly, Carl, without that sheriff down there, we never could have done it."

Those clouds Tanner had misread had edged well down across the mountain rims and were gradually moving southward into the path of the riders. Otherwise, the day was brilliantly colored—warm without being hot—and the humid air became increasingly heavy and fragrant.

After watching those clouds for a long time, the youngest cowboy, the man to whom no one ever paid much attention, made another observation that drew the heads of his older companions around.

"A man is born wet an' keeps gettin' wet on and off until the day he dies, and maybe he gets wetted on then, too, for all anyone knows."

Carl and Dutch Meier laughed. No one else did. Tanner might have, except that he was deep in private thought. He could guess what Frank was thinking, but with Frank a man could never be sure, because his face seldom reflected his moods or thoughts. Since they were riding alongside one another, Tanner said, "Frank, as far as I know, no one ever said cowmen were wise, did they?"

Frank grinned. "No, not that I know of. One time my grandpappy told me a feller's biggest problem in this life is not to be a horse's ass more'n maybe ten or fifteen minutes out of every day. Then he told me that he doubted like hell if there was ever a man who lived that didn't exceed that by sometimes four or five hours, and sometimes men were horse's asses all their danged lives."

Tanner laughed. "Then I guess being one for only about a month isn't too bad, is it?"

They all laughed—and those big soiled clouds moved steadily toward them.

CHAPTER 17

The Agency

When the rain finally arrived, it was mixed with stinging particles of snow. But the heavens had been darkening for two days before the Rafter T range men got caught by it, and that was enough time to look for shelter.

During the worst of the storm, they holed up under some limestone bluffs, in caves large enough to hold twice as many men and horses as Tanner had with him.

They had trouble finding dry wood, and even more trouble finding something to shoot for their meals during the deluge, but they were resourceful men, and they were also inured to exactly this kind of hardship. They did not like it, but they would have liked it a lot less if there hadn't been plenty of horse feed beyond the limestone cliffs, and if Lew Brown had not shot a spike deer.

Once they got a cooking fire lighted, they did not allow it to die, because nearly all the wood they brought to the cave was wet and would only ignite if it were piled atop burning wood. In the process, it steamed and smoked.

On the third day, when they struck camp under a thin veil of gray and cheerless sky, they had smoke scent embedded in

154

their clothing, and until they found a creek to wash in, they also had smoke residue on their skin.

About their clothing they could do nothing, nor did that bother them very much; they had been living inside the same boots, britches, shirts, and hats for a long time. As long as they were out of doors, the rankness was hard to notice.

Four days later, with the sky steely clear, and with a brisk ground breeze rattling dry underbrush, they came down out of a heavy stand of virgin timber and started across the great plateau, which, on its far side, had a straggling set of old log structures occupied by the Indian Agency.

Despite the delay caused by the storm, they made better time riding northward than they had made previously, going the other way.

They were back in familiar country; the agency's boundary adjoined Rafter T range along a none-too-well-defined line. At one time or another, each of them had ridden the line, hunting strays or predators.

Long before they had the agency buildings in sight, they saw riders, some of whom were Indians—and some of whom were not; Tanner speculated that they were either traders or soldiers, but distance usually prevented him from making positive identifications, nor did he much care who they were.

When they came into the large parade ground with its dozens of buildings and its very tall whitewashed pole flying the national flag, Tanner headed directly for the largest log structure. Out front, on a roofed-over wide porch four or five men were idly watching their approach from slat-bottomed old chairs. They were civilians, except for one noncommissioned officer whose belt had an empty saber hanger and a holstered Colt.

Tanner swung off out front at the hitch rack, shoved gloves under his belt, nodded at the men watching him, and led his riders up onto the porch, where the sergeant fixed Tanner with an unsmiling expression of inquiry. Tanner recognized the man; he had been with Captain Bledsoe down at Tomkinsville two weeks ago.

Tanner was reaching for the door when the sergeant said, "If you want to see Captain Bledsoe, he's out on the reservation."

Tanner hauled the door open as he said, "I came to see Colonel Stuart," and led his men into the large outer room, where an enlisted man at a table glanced up, watched all the Rafter T men come in, and rose as he said, "What can I do for you?"

"We'd like to see Colonel Stuart," Tanner answered, and saw the orderly's look of quick curiosity.

"He's busy. Tell me what it's about and I'll talk to him."

Frank and Lew regarded the orderly from unsmiling faces as Tanner replied, "It's about some Rafter T cattle, and some In'ians."

The corporal's eyes showed understanding. "All right. What's your name?"

"Tanner."

The orderly's expression underwent an abrupt change. "Tanner," he murmured, looking intently at one after another of them. "All right. Have seats and I'll go see what I can do."

When the orderly departed, Lew Brown said, "I guess Mr. Bledsoe or that sergeant on the porch already got in their licks about us."

They did not go to the wall benches but remained standing. Dutch Meier built and lit a cigarette, and Carl strolled toward a wall hung with pictures of officers in glassed frames and stood studying them until the orderly returned.

"In a little while," the corporal told Tanner. "Have seats."

They still remained standing. Bledsoe's sergeant came in and leaned to murmur something into the orderly's ear, then went back out onto the porch without glancing at any of the range men. The corporal eyed Tanner askance but said nothing until a lean, hard-faced, graying man with a colonel's shoulder straps appeared in a doorway. The corporal rose and said, "That's Will Tanner, Colonel. Those are his men. Sergeant Murphy's on the porch."

The officer fixed Tanner with his hawkish gaze, then curtly said, "Mr. Tanner, come into the office."

They all filed in, and as the colonel turned from behind his desk and saw his office full of range men, his mouth flattened slightly and the testiness of his gaze became more pronounced, but he sat down and said, "Be seated. What is it, Tanner—Indians stole some of your cattle?"

Tanner remained standing. He had been to the agency before but ordinarily dealt with civilians and one or two officers who were responsible for making gate counts of the cattle he delivered. He had seen Colonel Stuart before, but this was the first time they had ever met.

"They didn't steal cattle, Colonel; I gave them some cattle."

Stuart leaned back, staring at Tanner. "I understand that's what you told Captain Bledsoe when he caught up with you. That's commendable. But there seems to be some doubt that you gave those cattle to the Indians."

Frank came around slowly. So did Lew and Carl and Dutch. Tanner said, "Are you saying, Colonel, that someone has called me a liar?"

Colonel Stuart rose from his desk before replying and went to the far wall to open two windows, then returned to his desk. But this time he leaned forward and did not sit down.

"I don't believe I said that, Tanner."

"What did you say?"

Stuart was an incisive, hard career soldier. He continued to lean there, gazing directly at Tanner for a long time before speaking again. "Tanner, the best way we have of keeping

ourselves posted about conditions on the reservation is
through informers. This reservation covers hundreds of
miles, and we do not have the forces to patrol it properly. So
we use informers. The story we got was that two Indians
raided your range, you came onto the reservation—which,
incidentally, is not allowed—found some of those cattle, and
drove them off. Then you went after the thieves. Would you
say that was an approximation of what happened, Tanner?''

"I just told you, Colonel. I gave cattle to those Indians.
Now, I'm up here to tell you that—and to also tell you that if
you send soldiers after those two In'ians, I'm going to look
them up, too, and if they need help when the soldiers arrive,
we'll give it to 'em.''

Colonel Stuart continued to lean on the desk top looking at
Tanner, but now his hard, uncompromising features became granite-hard. "That would be a very great mistake,
Mr. Tanner. In the first place, white men are not allowed on
the reservation unless they have authorization from my office. In the second place—''

"Colonel, that's a boot that fits both feet. No soldiers or
agency people are allowed on my range without my permis-
sion—but I've seen them down there many times.''

"That is different, Mr. Tanner. For us to police this
place, the men are required to go anywhere.''

"It's no different at all, Colonel. I've used In'ians for
range riders. I'll go on using them like that whenever I need
hands, and whenever they come looking for work . . . and if
you send men onto my range to make trouble for my riders. . . . Colonel, *that* would be a very great mistake.''

Frank suddenly said, "Colonel, how's it come you don't
feed your In'ians?''

Stuart straightened up from the desk, reddening. "Who
the hell are you? My business is with Will Tanner.''

"I'm Will Tanner's top hand," stated Frank, not yielding

under the army officer's fierce look. "I'd like an answer to my question."

Instead of replying, Colonel Stuart glared at Tanner. "Anything to be said, you will say, Mr. Tanner."

Lew Brown said, "Crap!" and the officer's voice was immediately raised in an outraged shout. "Orderly!"

The corporal appeared in the doorway. "Yes sir!"

"Get these men out of here!"

No one moved except Tanner. He stepped forward until he and the officer had the width of the desk separating them, then Tanner said, "Colonel, you're dead set on trouble, aren't you? All right; I'll oblige you. First off, if Bledsoe is on the reservation, my guess is that he's lookin' for Walt and Ben. If he hauls them in here, I will swear that I gave those cattle to them. And the reason I did that was because you *do* have starvin' In'ians, and you're not doing a damned thing about it. Colonel, starving In'ians have broken out before and gone on rampages, killing people, burning ranches, raising general hell. I'm going to write to every damned newspaper I can get an address for and warn of the danger of a mass breakout right here at your agency. I'm goin' to ask the newspapers to send people out here to talk to the In'ians— the starving ones. You want trouble, damn you, I'll give you a gutful!"

Stuart's voice was almost a shout. "There are no starving Indians on this reservation! You have been lied to by renegades, and you have been foolish enough to believe them!"

"Not by a damned sight," exclaimed Tanner. "I've had to live with these redskins a hell of a lot longer than you have; they don't fool me, nor any other range men in this country. *You have starving In'ians!*"

The white-faced orderly, still in the doorway, said, "Sir, do you want me to get the guard?"

For five seconds there was absolute silence, then Colonel Stuart glared at the orderly. "Get out and close the door!"

The corporal moved swiftly to obey. As soon as the door was closed, the officer stepped to the window directly behind his desk and opened that window, too. Then he faced around, still red in the face, making a great effort to keep his voice down as he said, "Mr. Tanner, no one knows where those two Indians are. Captain Bledsoe has been looking for them for several days. If they are on the reservation, our informers have not seen them." The colonel saw Frank and Lew Brown exchange a look and ignored that. "All right, Tanner . . . I will personally supervise an investigation. If I find any Indians without food, you have my word the situation will be corrected. As I told you, I don't have the staff to look after everything. We do the best we can with what is available."

Tanner stood gazing at the officer a long time without speaking. Unlike Colonel Stuart, Tanner's anger never got to the shouting stage, and it lasted a lot longer. He turned toward the door and halted with his hand on the latch.

"Are you going to bring Walt and Ben in if your men find them?"

Stuart had already made his judgment of Will Tanner. "Will you give it to me in writing that you gave those cattle to them?"

"You got a pencil and some paper?"

"The orderly has in the other room. Give it to him."

"All right. But that don't answer my question."

"When I have it from you that they did not steal any cattle from you, I'll recall Captain Bledsoe and his squad. There has been a misunderstanding, is all. . . . No, I will not have the Indians brought in if we find them."

Tanner walked out into the larger room where the nervous orderly was sitting at a table. The last man to leave the colonel's office was Lew Brown, and he looked back at Colonel Stuart for a moment, then closed the door.

Tanner growled at the orderly for paper and a pencil.

When they were produced, he wrote his note, tossed down the pencil, and straightened up as the burly, grizzled sergeant entered the big room with four armed soldiers.

Tanner and his riders eyed the armed soldiers, who glared back, and Tanner started for the front door. The sergeant blocked his way, mean in the face and truculent.

Tanner did not stop. He shouldered the sergeant aside, heard the snarl, and started to turn, but Dutch Meier, who was the sergeant's equal in built and heft, had already reached for the sergeant. He spun him off balance. The sergeant's knees struck a bench from behind, and he suddenly sat down.

The armed soldiers closed up to bar the doorway. Colonel Stuart abruptly appeared in his office doorway, saw what was in the making, and roared.

"What are you men doing in here?"

No one answered until the orderly spoke in a reedy voice. "I sent for them, sir."

"Corporal! I distinctly told you not to call the guard!"

"Sir—"

"Get out!" thundered the colonel at the confused armed soldiers. "Out! Sergeant! Stand up when a superior officer enters a room!"

The noncommissioned officer had been struggling to rise. He got to his feet and stood stiffly, facing Colonel Stuart.

"Leave this building, Sergeant! Take a horse, go find Captain Bledsoe, and tell him by my orders he is to discontinue his present assignment and report back here to me at once!"

Tanner walked out onto the porch, where the idlers were swiftly leaving their chairs. As the soldiers and the sergeant came outside, the loafers were already walking briskly across the large parade ground.

Colonel Stuart went as far as the doorway and remained there watching Tanner and his men turn to ride southward across the big compound. When they were far enough along for him to be sure they would continue riding, he said, "Orderly! Go over to the doctor's office, get one of those sulphur candles he uses, bring it back here, and burn it in my office. . . . Even Indians don't smell that bad."

The sky was darkening again, but there was turbulence high up, which shredded clouds and made the Rafter T men suspect that it was not going to storm, at least not till they reached the home ranch, and if it stormed then, they would not care.

Lew Brown let out a big breath and felt for his tobacco sack as he turned toward Frank. "If you'd have offered to bet money that old son of a bitch back there wouldn't back down, I'd not have bet with you. For a while I figured we was all going to end up in his stockade."

Frank was buttoning his coat and, looking off toward the wild, distant mountains, he ignored what Lew had said. "That damned captain couldn't have found them anyway," he said. Then he looked at the other riders, squared up in his saddle, waited until Lew had lit up, and added, "Now, by gawd, the holiday is over; you'n everyone else can start working again."

Lew turned very slowly to stare at the top hand, but he did not say a word.